ALL SYSTEMS SNOW

BY

DEREK McFADDEN

8 Tales of Christmas Times

The
Tinsel & Twists
Series

All Systems Snow

Copyright 2023

Derek McFadden

Published by
Papillon du Père Publishing

PAPILLON DU PÈRE
PUBLISHING

ISBN: 978-1-915221-16-2

ALSO BY
DEREK McFADDEN

Novel

What Death Taught Terrence

Tinsel & Twists **Series**

The Santa Claus Agreement

All Systems Snow: *8 Tales of Christmas Times*

Short Stories

What Eternity Taught Eve

The Last Christmas Gift

Written by the Victors

Nonfiction

Prose from a Grandson to a Senior Fellow

DEDICATION

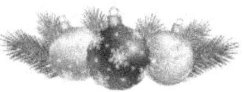

For Katie-blue. This is one of your Christmas presents, 2023. I have always considered any time we get to spend together a true gift.

And for Monica. With thanks for all the close reads and for catching the pie ending!

Also, as always, for Pop.

D

CONTENTS

ALSO BY DEREK MCFADDEN V

DEDICATION VII

CONTENTS.. IX

THE LAST CHRISTMAS GIFT.. 1

CARRIE CLARK'S CHRISTMAS WISH 27

THE BELL-RINGER 45

THE FAIRNESS OF LIFE 49

WRITTEN BY THE VICTORS: A VIGNETTE 65

WHO WE'LL BE.. 73

A WINDOW INTO THE FUTURE 91

THE UNCERTAIN NEW DAY OF HAROLD THE RAINDROP 117

BONUS STORY WHAT ETERNITY TAUGHT EVE........................123

THANKS FOR READING.. 149

AUTHOR BIO.. 151

ALSO AVAILABLE 153

    What Death Taught Terrence 153

    More Christmas fun in... the *Tinsel & Twists* series 157

    And more Christmas fun in... 161

    And even more Christmas fun in... 165

    The Bells of Christmas II..167

    13 by 11 An Anthology 173

THE LAST CHRISTMAS GIFT

I know this is a ride to nowhere. To no*when*, actually.

A ferry ride with no destination. Or, at least, no destination that still exists in the way modern society understands existence. The truth is, I'm trying to find my way back to a place I once knew and loved. A place in which I was always assured of being both known and loved.

"Sweetheart! It's so wonderful to see you! Merry Christmas! Come in, come in! Pop just took a batch of cookies out of the oven, and we bought a new carton of egg nog—just for you because we knew you were coming over!"

My grandmother's greeting plays like a well-loved record in my head. I'm searching for that place this December afternoon, the day before Christmas, in spite of the fact that someone else I don't know owns my grandparents' house now, and they've both been gone almost twenty years. In spite of the fact that, when our ferry reaches the shore, there won't be anyone I love waiting to pick me up. No one to spend Christmas with me. To eat chocolates out of an advent calendar whose dates are marked by a little stuffed-animal mouse you'd move from one date to the next to the next until today's date came to be.

That's because I'm headed for Christmas in the 1990s. A simpler time for me. Likely a simpler time for the world as a whole, but that, I concede, is a broad generalization. It was a time of calm and peace and joy in my life, however, in spite of my cerebral palsy (which turns my right foot too far right and gives people reason to doubt my relevance).

I'm not so much aiming for the *actual* Christmases of the 90s, which—on some level—I know are gone for good. Holidays, by their very nature, are ethereal. Singular moments here one day, gone the next, to stay gone forever. No, I'm searching for the *feelings* those family gatherings left imprinted within me.

Call this a recovery mission.

Nostalgia is what I'm after this early afternoon when no one else appears dumb enough to have paid money to ride a ferry in the middle of a frothy, choppy Puget Sound. An angry Seattle winter rain (is it coming down sideways or is that just my perception?) pelts the otherwise empty boat's windows, the droplets impacting then streaking down the windows out of which I can see little beyond a permanently gray world.

***

I took this very same ferry ride countless times as a kid. We're talking in the hundreds, maybe even the thousands. Sometimes with my parents. Many times with my younger brother, Ben, four years my junior and the first of us boys to marry the love of his life. (I suppose, in order to marry such a love, you must first find her, a feat I've yet to manage. I thought I'd done it, though, with April.) Many of those sailings were packed full, the car-deck teeming with automobiles and each pair of rectangular seats in the upstairs main cabin filled. So the fact that this ferry is empty, save for its crew—because someone needs to drive this thing and ensure we don't run aground—and I appear to be the only paying passenger aboard is something of a shock to me.

It was my mom who first floated the idea, about a month ago at Thanksgiving, that I board this boat today.

"Why would I do that, Mom?" I asked as we ate too much turkey and watched too much football. "Especially by myself." While I *had* ridden the ferry by myself many times in the past, while I *could* do it, everyone who knew me was well aware I frowned at the thought.

"For old time's sake," my mom said.

Initially, I pushed back against the suggestion. "There's nothing and no one across that water for me, Mom. Not anymore. They're gone."

"They're not gone, Travis. Anyone who still lives within your heart is never truly *gone*."

It was only after having the idea unexpectedly seconded by my therapist, Melody, the following week that I relented.

"I think you should do it!" she said excitedly.

"You what? Why?"

"You may not find your grandparents at the end of that boat ride." On this, she was undoubtedly correct. "But you'll be able to commune with memories and make some new ones while you're at it. I'd wager you'll find some joy in it."

"You'd wager I'll find some joy in it? Do you wanna put your money where your mouth is, Doc?" I challenged.

"It's not *that* kind of wager. But that boat trip is the homework I'm giving you over the holidays, and I expect you to report back and tell me how it went when we see each other again after the New Year."

I left Melody's office, shaking my head and doubting. But taking this ride was my homework. As she said, we'd discuss its effectiveness—along with how many holiday pounds I put on (spoiler alert: too many)—when the calendar flipped to January.

"Enjoy your holidays, Travis!" Melody called after me as I shut her office door behind me.

I'd wondered then if I'd ever actually enjoyed my holidays since my grandparents died. Both of them from cancer. Papa went first, after a six-year-long battle, followed by Grandma, six years later, who lost a battle she kept private until her collapsing in the grocery store meant she couldn't keep the thing that would end her private any longer.

***

On this nearly empty boat (it's *too* empty! This same short voyage was packed full of souls on past holidays—I saw it with my own not-great eyes), I again question the wisdom of this "assignment."

I take a seat on one of the many available bench-seats. Ferryboat etiquette dictates that no one will sit either with or on the seat across from anyone they don't know, which means this pair of bench-seats is all mine for the next twenty minutes. As I settle onto the soft bench and gaze out the window at a quintessential pacific northwest Christmas—the sky dark with clouds pouring rain—the usual perfunctory announcements I've heard a thousand times crackle over the vessel's loudspeaker. Which is garbled and staticky and not all that loud.

Life preservers at the front and back of the boat, if needed (sure hope we never, ever need them). Follow all crew instructions (as if I was planning to mutiny on Christmas Eve!). Enjoy your ride from Edmonds, Washington, across the Puget Sound to the small town of Kingston. (Okay, so this last announcement wasn't quite as involved as I've written it; all they said was "Enjoy the sailing," but a writer needs to fit exposition in somewhere.)

***

This isn't my first Christmas without my grandparents. It's not even the first Christmas I'll technically spend alone. I'm no introvert, trust me, so it's not like I *want* to spend it alone, but convincing people to hang with you on Christmas is a tough ask, especially when they don't have a connection to you beyond the workplace, or maybe they're an acquaintance with whom you're friendly but distant, as society requires these days. But this is the most conspicuous of all of my "alone" Christmases for one simple reason: I'm going through a break-up.

Writing that little phrase takes real guts. Guts I haven't had until now. That's right, I've been trying to admit this truth to myself for two months now: *I'm going through a break-up.* But it's refused recognition. Or, more accurately, my mind wouldn't allow it to cross the necessary synapses in my brain and *be* recognized.

As the reality of the break-up began to dawn on me six months ago (this was, after all, a process), I considered therapy for the first time. Not physical therapy, mind you—of which I've had more than my share, born as I was with cerebral palsy and a body inherently wound tight—

5

I'm talking about the kind of therapy one gets when things don't feel right ... upstairs.

I first met my therapist, Melody, on a Tuesday afternoon.

"So what brings you here, Travis?" she'd asked, looking at me over a pair of big glasses.

At that exact moment, I didn't really know. Or, if I knew, I didn't want to say.

"I love my girlfriend, and she suggested I get into therapy."

"Ah. What's her name?"

"April."

"Is she in counseling, too?"

I nodded. "She thinks I could get a lot out of it. So I'm here."

Melody leveled her gaze directly at me for the first time. "And what do *you* think?"

"What do I ...?"

"Think? Yes, what do you think? Is April right?"

"I hope so. Otherwise, I don't know what I'm doing here."

Hearing this fact escape my mouth brought a twinge to my chest, and I didn't know why.

"Travis, what do *you* want and expect out of our time together?" Melody challenged me.

"I don't know," I lied.

"Yes, you do," she pressed. "I suspect you do know, or you wouldn't be here. What do *you* want?"

"I want to go back in time," I said after a long moment.

"How's that?" Melody removed a pencil from behind her ear and wrote something on a pad of paper to her right. Something, I imagine, like *Has grandiose but impossible ideas about life.* "Why do you want to go back in time?"

"Because ..." I thought about it. "Because there was a time when people loved me, and that time has *clearly* passed, and I'd like to get back to it. I want to go back in time. You understand, don't you, Doc?"

"I understand you might not feel good right now, Travis. But we'll work on fixing that. It'll take time and effort on both our parts, but we'll fix it. Together. But to get there means your cooperation. This won't work unless you give me your complete cooperation. Do I have it?"

You either do this—and do it right—or April will leave you, I'd thought back then. That couldn't happen.

"You have it, Doc," I agreed.

I've been seeing Melody twice a week ever since. Yet, as helpful as my counseling has been, it *did not* and *cannot* save my relationship. April is gone. Has been for about a month or so now. We keep saying we'll find time to celebrate "our" Christmas together, but I know I won't see her until the New Year at the earliest.

Effectively, I'm holding onto something that is no longer a *something.*

The ship has sunk. And I'm its loyal captain, duty bound to go down with my doomed charge.

***

Taking the advice of both my mom and my therapist, I board a boat I've likely been on countless times (although, who's to say? All these vessels look the same, and it's difficult for me to read the name affixed to the vessel's front both because my eyes are not—and never have

7

been—good, and on account of the windblown mist-rain that acts as a spray this winter day, buffeting me as I enter the cabin), I'm going back in time. In a manner of speaking, anyway. Or at least as far back in time as modern technology will allow me to go.

Thinking back on all the Christmases I spent with my grandparents, something else Melody has asked me to do as a kind of homework, I realize only now that I don't remember each holiday as a distinct entity. As much as I'd like to, I don't. Rather, they run together; one runs into the next, which runs into the Christmas after it. It is as though my usually unimpeachable memory, in an attempt to catalogue everything—from Papa's refrigerator cookies to the playing of Stan Borreson records (a uniquely *us* Christmas tradition important only to our family) to Grandma's intentionally bad carol-singing to my favorite Christmas gifts of all time—in an attempt to remember it all, my memory has abridged my holidays. And, in only recording the basics, my memory has squandered what it was about Christmas that once made the holiday essential.

Or maybe I'm just getting older and the things that mattered to me when I was a kid just don't matter anymore. Maybe it's that simple.

My thoughts can't help but return to the emptiness of this boat. An emptiness I might understand if this sailing came early in the morning. But smack in the midst of a cold afternoon, I don't get it.

I should be here with April, I think. If she were here, everything would be different. Better.

I'm glancing out the window as this thought occurs to me. Maybe I should refute it, but I'm too tired to try. A break-up takes a lot out of a guy.

"So you're feeling sorry for yourself? That's what you're doing now? On Christmas Eve, of all days?"

I *know* that voice. Only one man could ever speak to me in such a cutting yet insightful manner.

I turn from the window ...

To see my papa.

A young version of my papa—still sporting the black hair of my early childhood, hair that has yet to turn silver—is sitting across from me on an otherwise empty close-to-yellow bench-seat. He's wearing a plaid shirt under a "Kiss-The-Cook" apron. Not exactly ferry-riding clothing, but at least it fits the holiday. I'd be willing to bet there's a bottle of Tums either in a pocket of his blue jeans or stowed inside the winter coat that he wears, unzipped. ("It's not *that* cold," he'd often say.)

Is he really sitting there, or am I just overtired?

"Pop?"

"Yeah, it's me."

"How?"

"How isn't important," he says, looking me straight in the eye, the intensity of his gaze off-putting. Papa only ever looked at me this way when he was trying to hammer home a point I'd failed to grasp, or when he thought I was doing something *very* wrong and he needed to step in.

""I feel so alone," I say.

"Uh-huh," Pop says, but what he's really saying without saying it is: *What does that mean to you?*

I don't respond to this unasked question. Instead, I say something to my papa that I never thought I'd get to say again. "Merry Christmas, Pop."

Just this phrase chokes me up. I fight to keep the tears from coming. Swallow down the lump in my throat.

"Merry Christmas, kid." He pauses, changes the subject. "I think we've got work to do."

"How's that? I mean, how can that be?"

"*How* I'm here is not important," Pop explains. "What's important is *why*."

I'm thrown off. I don't know why. Other than I'd definitely thought that, the next time I saw Pop, gone nearly two decades now, the next time I wished him a merry Christmas, the mood would be celebratory. We'd be reunited to stay.

"Okay ... so, why are you here, Pop?" I ask.

"I'm here because you need me. But let's not worry about that just yet. Tell me about your life."

"Tell you about my life?"

"Yeah. What have I missed since I've been gone? Tell me all of it." He takes from his coat pocket a folded section of his newspaper. "And, while you talk and I listen, I've got a crossword to do. I hope you don't mind if I interrupt you if I have any questions for you. Or if I get stuck on a clue."

Strange. But okay: after all, why disagree when your long-dead grandfather shows up on Christmas Eve and tells you he's shown up because you need him? Foolhardy to argue the point! These parameters agreed to, I begin the story of my life since his passing, and Pop begins his puzzle as he'd always begun every one of his crossword puzzles: hopeful.

***

Pop, the man who taught me how to swim over many successive summer vacations—"Kick your feet, Travis! You're handicapped, but you still *have* legs. Don't forget about 'em. Use 'em. Kick those feet!"—and the man who taught me how to love without ever *trying* to teach me how to love—*Treat every girl I date the way Pop treated Grandma, I'll be fine,* I remember thinking on many a date—the man I thought could never die because heroes never died ... that man passed away when I was just a week shy of my twenty-first birthday. Back then, my life was infinite and limitless as it stretched out before me. *Sure, I might be handicapped, but I can do anything I put my mind to. I won't be climbing a mountain anytime soon, mind you,* I thought. *But that's never been a dream of mine, anyway. The things I want to do, whatever those things end up being, I will do.* My parents, and especially my paternal grandparents, had hammered this idea home for years. In the years immediately prior to Pop's passing, it was taking hold.

Since then, I've learned the truth.

And I've learned that the truth hurts.

"I don't know where to start, Pop," I tell him, my head in my hands.

He doesn't look up from his crossword, which he's donned his glasses to read. "Start at the beginning. That way, you can tell the whole story." Though he's still looking at the newspaper, now I can glimpse the hint of a smile playing on his mustachioed lips.

"Okay. Well, first thing's first, Pop. It hasn't all been great since you've been gone."

Now he places the crossword facedown on his lap. Looks into my eyes. "You think if your life was running smoothly, Travis, that I'd be here right now? Tell me from the beginning. If I have questions, I'll cut in and ask them. But you're a writer, aren't you?" I *had* published a novel about a year ago. If doing so made you a writer, then I *was* a writer. "All writers are storytellers. Tell me your story," he repeats, firmer this time.

Alright, I think. From the beginning.

***

"Pop, you died on a Saturday in May, only a week before my twenty-first birthday. I don't know why, maybe it's out of some sort of morbid curiosity, but ever since, I've wondered on what day of the week I would die. That twenty-first birthday was the saddest birthday I've ever experienced. That first beer I'd been waiting to have with you and its accompanying steak didn't taste too good because, even though Dad was there, you weren't, Pop.

"After you died, Pop, Grandma got mean. I'm sure you were watching, so you had to see it, but she went from the happy-go-lucky Grandma I knew to a suddenly sour, self-centered wench. I'm sorry. I know you love her, and we're not supposed to speak ill of the dead, but it's the truth."

At this, Pop nods in acknowledgment. *Proceed*, the gesture says, as he grunts his disapproval with one of his puzzle's more difficult clues.

I go on. Speaking of this particular time of year, I tell Pop how Christmas, formerly my favorite holiday, was never the same after he passed. Grandma did her best, of course. Our whole family did. But when someone dies in a family, and especially when that someone was the glue that kept a family together, there's only so much *anyone* can do to hold together a now-tattered quilt of relations. Within a couple years, the tradition of holding Christmas Day at Pop and Grandma's house ended. It did so unceremoniously. No one came right out and said, "This is the last year we're doing Christmas here." Had someone actually said this, in as many words, I'm confident an outcry would have resulted. Instead, it was never directly discussed; we just knew we didn't want to spend an hour or more in a ferry line every December 25th, and my dad has spent every Christmas since hosting a subsection of the large crowd who used to congregate at Grandma and Papa's place.

Now Pop looks annoyed. I stop talking a second.

"What's wrong, Pop?" I ask.

"Two things," he grumbles. "First of all, I don't need a history lesson on our family."

"You don't?"

"No. I was in it before you were. What I need is for you to be honest with yourself."

"About what?"

"About what it is you're actually doing on this boat." He pauses, fixes me with a look that says *You can lie to yourself, Travis, but you better not lie to me.* "And second," he continues, "I need your help."

"With what?"

"With this damn clue. I can't make heads or tails of it. Four across. The clue is *bathday cake*, whatever the hell that means. S, blank, blank, blank."

Ah, he's mad at his crossword, too. I've seen him work many a crossword before, and he's continually furrowing his brow at this one. I honor Pop's second request first because it's the easiest to carry out. "Soap," I tell him.

"Soap?"

"Yeah, you know ... like a cake of soap."

"Boy, you are pretty smart, aren't you?" He pencils this in and smiles when he realizes it works.

"I like to think so," I say.

"So then, what the hell are you doing on this boat?"

I sit back, letting myself sink into the bench-seat, and consider this. "I don't know. I'm depressed—"

"That much is obvious."

"I'm *depressed*." I'm talking louder now, and I've made sure to emphasize the word. It isn't merely a word or simply a state I've been mired in recently. The fact is, depression is now one of the major tenets of my personality. I hate it, but I can't seem to escape it.

"Shit, we've all been depressed. You think when I was in Korea, scared shitless, that I wasn't also goddamned depressed? 'Course I was. Could have been home with my young family on Christmas, for example, but instead I was half a damn world away contemplating the killing of other human beings. How, if I didn't kill them, they might well kill me."

"Jeez, Pop, if you don't want me to tell you the story of my life since you've been gone—"

"I *do* want you to tell me that story. But I want you to start from *your* beginning and focus on what matters most to *you*. This is only a twenty-minute boat ride, after all."

I lean forward, placing my hands on my knees. "Okay … okay. So, I'm not sure what matters to me anymore, Pop. I used to know. I used to be *certain* of what mattered to me. But then …"

"But then what?" Pop pencils in a crossword answer as I begin to wonder *What is this?* My papa returned to human form on a magical Christmas Eve, or is it simply another session with Melody?

"But then April gave up on me. On us."

"Your relationship ended, is what you're saying?"

"Yeah. That's right."

Maybe he'd oversimplified the thing. April and I had a vibrant and varied history together, from our trips to Disneyland to the many times we'd held each other up when one or the other of us was ruled by feelings we didn't fully understand. Be they depression, manic joy, or apprehension and anxiety. But he *is* right. My relationship has ended. Even admitting this much stirs my feelings like a chef would stir an indigestible, unwanted pot of soup. Not Pop's, though, my favorite chef of all time; he liked to make turkey soup for the holidays. And we loved consuming it.

"What do you want, Travis? For the world to feel sorry for you?" he challenges.

"No, no, I don't want that. What I want is ..." I pause, and only then do I realize I've misspoken. "Okay, so maybe I do want the world to feel *a little* bad for me. To realize what I had and how ... how *good* it was. And all I had to go through to get it! And how sad I am that it's gone forever."

"That's asking an awful lot of the world," Pop says. There's no judgment in his tone. But there *is* honesty. "And, truthfully ..." He reaches into his coat pocket and extracts a Tums tablet, something I'd seen him do so many times in life; heartburn enjoyed shadowing him. "Truthfully, it's asking an awful lot of yourself, too. Nostalgia is one thing. I'm all for a trip into the past. But when you take those trips, you have to be absolutely clear-eyed about where and when it is you're going and what your objective will be once you get there. What it is you *want*."

Pop was so good at this. He'd always been so good at this. The taking aside of his grandchildren and, honestly, anyone who was his charge, and telling them—always quietly, so as not to embarrass them, but always dead-straight, and right when they needed to hear it—how life worked. Before my brother and I, he'd done the same for my father and my uncle. And my older cousins, my uncle's kids, the eldest of whom is a decade my senior. Neither of us is kids anymore.

"The whole world can't stop and mourn a lost relationship with you. The world stops for absolutely no one; that's the same thing your grandmother wanted when she lost me—and she didn't get it, either. So what is it you really want, kid?" He's looking at me purposefully over his glasses.

"I want to know what it feels like not to have my cerebral palsy! I'm always walking in molasses. Other people move around with a confidence and a freedom I'll never know."

"Did I say I was a genie, Travis?"

"What? No."

"Then why would you continue to ask me for things I can't give you? I'm here to *help* you. Not to transform your life into some unrealistic fantasy. We each are given the life we're given. That's what we get. No more, no less. And, sure, people complain about their lots in their lives all the time. It's natural, part of being human. You ever known anyone able to do what you're asking?"

I think hard, my head resting against the back of my bench-seat. All the while knowing the answer is no. "What about rags to riches stories? They happen all the time."

Pop gives me a look that says *You're kidding me, right?* He doesn't need to actually say that if I'm not gonna take this seriously, he'll go back to his crossword.

"Well, they happen all the time in the movies," I correct.

"Is your life a movie?"

"No."

Sometimes, I might *want* to be in a movie, though. The charming star. I won't lie. Specifically, in one of those romantic comedies where the good guy—me, of course—always gets the girl in the end, and the biggest problem the couple has on their path to matrimonial and forever-after bliss is when the absent-minded guy forgets he's made a date with his beloved and inadvertently stands her up waiting for him at a fancy restaurant, leading to the twenty minutes in the film during which our guy thinks he's lost the girl for good, only to find out that, no, he hasn't. And he *won't.* Because it's a movie, the modern equivalent of a fairy tale, and Hollywood demands its heroes succeed, by any means necessary. Meaning that, no matter how much of a failure I feel like in real life, I couldn't fail in a movie.

"You trying to live a movie? Even though, Mr. Writer, you know your life isn't one?"

I don't want to tell him my reasoning, which I've just come by, and of which I'm not proud. He won't like it. *I* don't like it. So I stay quiet. Let him get to his point.

"Don't live a movie. Live the moment."

"Live the moment?" I say, skepticism reigning in both my voice and my countenance.

He nods.

"And how do I do that? I've never even heard that expression before. Unless you mean live *in* the moment?"

"I don't," Pop answers. "I said what I meant to say. *Live the moment.* It means to accept each moment in life as

17

it comes. To live *that* moment's reality in full. Don't get ahead of it. Try not to lag behind it. When another moment comes, only then do you move into that moment and live *its* reality."

As what he says soaks in, I glance out the window. A dread is prickling at the back of my neck. The same dread I felt when I *knew* April was about to end things. But this dread is upon me for an entirely new reason.

I can still barely see anything out the boat window. All I know for certain is how the trees on the shore we'll reach in another ten minutes or so are getting closer and closer. My time with Papa, whom I haven't seen in so, so long, is ebbing away, sifting through my fingers like the finest grains of white sand on the Hawaiian beach he always wanted to visit but never did. Never could. (Grandma brought his ashes with us on the trip we took after his death, and she spread about a quarter of them on that beach, in that saying, "He made it to Hawaii after all.")

"See, you're not doing it," Pop admonishes, and his gruff voice has me leaving Hawaii, and I'm back on the boat on a rainy Christmas Eve.

"Not doing what?"

"You're not living the moment, Travis. You're not here with me now. Hell, you're not even on this boat. You're thinking about Hawaii and how your grandmother spread my ashes on the beach because I'd asked her to, and how I wasn't there—I was there, by the way, you just couldn't see me—and how it hurt you that I wasn't there."

I can't deny it. Any of it. He *knows. Just as he always seemed to know when I was "fibbing," my grandmother would call it.* I nod. Hide my face. I don't want him to see how tears are collecting at and stinging the backs of my eyes.

I can't let them fall.

"I'm so lonely," I admit to my grandfather. The admission shocks me. I hadn't known I was going to fess up to my loneliness until the three-word phrase was well clear of my mouth, its gatekeeper the last six months or so. That phrase has wanted out for half a year but not been granted leave until now.

Being lonely is different than being alone. Worse, harder to admit.

"How come?" Pop asks. "Why are you so lonely?"

"All the people I love ... What's the point of loving people the way I do? Holding them close over the holidays? Holding them close in my heart *all the time*? Giving them my *whole* heart the way I do? All the people I love eventually leave me. And there's nothing I can do about it."

"Welcome to life, kid," Pop declares, without actually declaring *anything*.

It's the most matter-of-fact I've ever seen him. This man who loved to joke. Sarcasm ran in tandem with the blood in his veins. This was a man who, on a snipe hunt he himself organized one summer Saturday night for my brother and me, looked me dead in the face and told me he'd just seen a snipe, a real-life *snipe*, and when I said I hadn't seen it, he swore it *was right there*. I'd simply been looking the other way, the *wrong* way, and he hadn't managed to get my attention fast enough. Before the animal—which I, of course, didn't know was imaginary at the time—skittered away, back into its burrow.

Yes, Pop loved to joke. Which meant that when he fell into his *serious* mode, you stopped what you were doing and you listened. That's what my brother and I would do, anyway. Pop had us well trained.

"Did all the people you love leave you, too, Pop?" I ask him.

"No."

"See, I *knew* it. It's me. There's something wrong with me. Beyond the palsy, I mean. Something's *really* wrong. That's why people lea—"

"No," Pop continued, ignoring my interruption. "Everyone I love didn't leave me. Because sometimes ... sometimes, *I* had to leave them, even though I didn't want to, and even though the leaving hurt like hell."

***

Marked by black pilings, the dock looms mere minutes ahead. My time with Pop is drawing to a close. But it doesn't appear he has much more to say to me. He goes back to his crossword.

Giving all he's said the time it needs to sink in?

Only when he finishes the puzzle does he take off his glasses, put them back in his coat pocket, toss the newspaper section down on the seat next to him, and sigh deeply.

"I suppose I should ask you now," he says, "what it is you need from me?"

"What I *need* from you?"

"Sure. You think dead grandfathers appear to their living grandsons every day? *Sheesh!* That would merit some news coverage. I'm *here* because you need something from me. Haven't you figured that out already?"

I'm embarrassed to tell him I hadn't.

Above us, the ferry's not-so-great loudspeaker crackles back to life. "We are arriving at our destination. All passengers *must* disembark the vessel within five minutes. Thank you."

By all passengers, I guess that guy means me. Who else is there?

So, what *do* I need from Pop?

"When April told me we were done," I explain, "I hadn't expected it, though all the signs of a relationship in trouble and fracturing had been there—how she'd been pulling away from me, and everyone could see it *but* me, because I chose not to see it—I remember one thought dominated my mind."

"What thought was that, Travis?

"How, if April only knew what my papa was like. How he'd raised me to believe in myself but not to be cocky, to *appreciate* my disability—instead of seeing it as a constant disadvantage, the reason I *couldn't* do things. And how he'd taught me to live every moment as though it was the most important moment of my life, because each succeeding moment *is* the most important moment of my life ... That's what it means to live in the present ... Guess I lost sight of that a little. But if April could only know all of these things about the man who made me a man, she wouldn't be breaking up with me." I pause. Gather my few belongings. I didn't bring many things with me besides myself. But in this post-9/11 world, we're trained as a society to scan our spaces and make certain both that we aren't leaving anything behind and that *no one else* has left anything in their wake, either.

I sigh. Even as I say all that ... I know it's not exactly true. "Even if April knew you, Pop, even if she'd loved you as deeply as I did, *as I always will*, I s'pose we would still have ended the way we ended."

"You think? Why's that?" Pop rose to his feet with me, his newspaper in the crook of his arm.

"I guess relationships only work if two people are willing to do the work. Together. And I guess maybe I had trouble living the moment. I've had trouble with that sort of thing since forever. I've always looked ahead. To the next milestone in our relationship, the next big vacation. Our next dinner-and-a-movie date. That next trip to Disneyland."

"And April?"

"April was dealing with her own stuff. Anxiety. Which induced panic. Which brought on sickness. Which is why she couldn't live the moment, either. I wanted to help her, to be there for her in the way I thought I was supposed to, as a man, but ..." I couldn't say the rest. It hurt too much to admit.

"But what?" Pop pushes.

"But the way I give support ... gave support ... maybe it wasn't the particular kind of support April needed. I may never know what it was she needed ... not precisely, anyway. All I know is ... as much as I wanted to, I couldn't give it to her."

At this, I wobble on my feet. Stagger back. Reach for Pop's considerable girth, hug him around his belly, and I begin to sob.

"I didn't want it to end, Pop," I cry. "I didn't want *us* to end."

"No one ever does *want* endings, kid," Pop says. "No one ever does."

***

As I speak these words, my soul begins to lighten, a massive invisible weight lifting. The relationship is over, but it's not my fault. *It's not anyone's fault.* It just is. From now on, as best I can, I'm going to live the moment; not three moments ahead or five moments behind.

Out the window, a cloudy sky is beginning to truly darken. It's 4 p.m. The sun has exited on cue, and somewhere near The North Pole, Santa must be readying his goodie-laden sleigh for a long but well-planned flight. It occurs to me that Santa would know how to live in the moment. At the same time, my surroundings inside the boat begin to change. To transform. There's been no one aboard this boat for our entire short voyage; now the bench-seats around me fill with families eager for the coming holiday.

"What the ...?" I'm taken aback by the sudden appearance of others. "Where did all these people come from, Pop?"

"These people?" Pop smiles, sweeps his hand over the greater area in much the same way a model on his favorite gameshow, *The Price Is Right*, might if she were showing off a new car. I still watch that show. Not every day but most days. Precisely because he loved it. "These folks've been on this boat the whole time."

"Then how come I couldn't see them? Pop, the boat was empty. I'd swear to that fact under oath, counselor," I say, doing my best imitation of a frazzled witness on one of the many police procedurals that populated the TV landscape in Pop's day, and still do.

"Most people are only focused on themselves."

I look around. "And their phones."

"Same thing, some would argue. Either way, they don't see you. For you, it isn't a phone that's blocking the world." He's right. I'm the one person on this planet who still doesn't have a phone. "It's you—your turmoil, Travis. Until you could clear the turmoil in your mind, you weren't going to see any of these people."

We prepare to disembark. I'm in line behind a little girl of about eight and her parents, who are each carrying a not-so-small pile of gift-wrapped packages. The little girl begins to sing. Softly at first. But as she gains confidence, her voice grows louder. And, as the rest of us realize what's happening, we join her. An impromptu caroling session that started with Jingle Bells, and by the time the boat's crew has the doors open and we're exiting in earnest, we're on to Let It Snow.

When that second song finishes, Pop is in my ear again. "You know I can't go any further, right?"

"What?"

"This isn't my world anymore. It's yours now, Travis. As long as you live the moments as they come, you'll be just fine."

"No!" I want to cry. Not again! I can't lose my papa *again*. I want to cry, scream my protest. But I know it'll do no good. Pop has to go. I know it. He's come to help me, but his Christmas delivery has now been made.

I look to the sky and see the cold rain has been replaced by soft snow. Just as the little girl and we carolers had asked. *Did Papa do this?*

"Merry Christmas, kid." His last words to me fade on the breeze and the flurry of snowflakes dancing around me.

"Merry Christmas, Pop. Thanks for showing me what I was missing. Thanks for setting me straight."

***

Since I had to disembark—I had no choice—I decided to walk from the ferry dock up a few blocks and then ascend the steep hill leading to my grandparents' old house ...

Where I'd spent so much of my childhood.

Where I'd been so loved and appreciated.

But when I got to the house, what I saw wasn't *their* house. It wasn't the house where I'd spent so many Christmases, so many summers, so many late afternoons sleeping in, only to mock-annoy Papa with the news that I wanted him to make me breakfast. His rule was the kitchen closes at 10 a.m. Somehow, I always managed to get my order in around 9:58.

Which always made my grandmother smile. "He's not late, Dick," she'd say. "He got his order in on time."

I loved *that* house. But it isn't *that* house anymore. It's just a dwelling. Someone else's domicile. Where someone else's memories are being made now. Where *their* family will spend holidays and seasons.

I still have memories to make, I think. So many memories. *They just ... won't be made here.*

And that's okay.

With this thought, I turn and make my way back to the ferry dock for the short trip home, aware of the last Christmas gift my grandfather will ever give me. Aware that, though I cannot hold it in my hands, his gift is more valuable than any material possession ever could be. And I'll forever hold it deep in my heart.

CARRIE CLARK'S CHRISTMAS WISH

The last rays of a dying light glinted across and ambered the big sky over Montana as their source bedded down, succumbing to its daily demise. Off to liven and wake and shine on another part of the world readying to start its day.

I took in this view from the back-passenger window of my family's Honda Accord, a choice of car I'd always found ironic, considering how our family could hardly ever come to an accord on anything. Especially my parents. Like their choice of music in the car: Dad voted for country; Mom voted for silence.

I voted for neither, opting for family chat.

Mom almost always won because, as Dad would tell me once I'd grown to adulthood, "I liked sleeping in my bed a lot more than sleeping on the sofa downstairs." Even when delivering a quip that brimmed with sad, salient truth, my dad could get me chuckling.

Other contentious car-trip decisions included—but were definitely not limited to—choice of restaurant. Dad wanted a steakhouse. Mom said she wanted Dad to live longer, so she didn't want to clog his heart with all that fat from the red meat he loved. We'd be having fish.

At home, she would relent one day a week, maybe, and Dad would smile as he cut into his roadhouse ribeye. Dad loved baseball. Mom wanted to chuck a baseball at his head for the suggestion. In fun, she assured me.

So the fact that Mom and Dad had agreed to take me and my older sister, Sharon (several years my senior) at all still amazed me. But I didn't question them. Curiosity never killed our cat; we never had one. Yet it could mortally wound any chance we still had to be a family. Questioning my parents tended not to make things any clearer or better for me, anyway. Instead, doing so, especially at an ill-timed moment, would throw life itself into doubt.

"Mom, why do you and Dad fight so much?" I would sometimes ask. "I don't like it."

"I don't like it, either, Carrie," my mother would often say. "But your father and I love each other."

"You do?" This puzzled me.

We talked quietly on our cross-country trip while Mom drove and Dad slept in the passenger seat and Sharon slept next to me.

"We always have loved each other," said Mom. "But we're both human. And relationships are hard. They take a lot of time to get right and ... and a willingness to work together."

When you're six years old and your mother is *that* frank with you, two things happen. Or at least they happened for me. I understood, in a way no child that young ever should, the unfairness of real life. And I also understood the draw towards fantasy and fairytales and stories and books. I could read by the next year, then by the time I was eleven, I could read *everything*, I happily lost myself in those books, with my mother's encouragement. My father's encouragement was by indifference.

Sharon was a huge help in my learning to read. Just before I started first grade, she came into my room, sat down on my bed, and asked me, "What do you really want to learn this year, Carrie?"

"To read!" I said, excited at the prospect. I was so excited I nearly threw my covers off. I wanted to know what was inside those books Mom was always reading. With as much time as she spent reading, it had to be good.

Sharon smiled. "Reading is fun! I'll tell you what, how about you and I take one night each week—how about Thursdays?—and I'll help you learn how to read?"

"Really? Would you really do that?"

"I would. I will. It won't be easy, and you might get frustrated with me sometimes, but by the end of this year, you'll be reading. You may not want to read Mom's books, though."

"Why not?"

"They're mostly romances," Sharon revealed.

"What're romances?"

"A whole lot of kissing."

"Ew, yuck."

Sharon was right. No romances for me. Romances were for old people.

***

Our neighborhood library was my favorite place to go on weekends. Beginning when I was eight. I'd arrive there Saturday morning after the cartoons on TV were over, and I'd stay for hours, until the librarian, a Ms. Tomlin, came over to me at my favorite reading table to tell me the building was about to close. She looked just like I imagined a librarian *would* look: brown hair done up in a bun, giant glasses dominating half her face, a pleasant smile ruling the other half.

"See you tomorrow, Carrie," she'd say at the end of each Saturday, her voice somehow still chipper after eight hours of quiet work behind her desk. She didn't talk much in that hushed library. No one did. Maybe the quiet explained her affinity for the job itself. "I hope you're enjoying that book."

"Oh, I am!" I'd say without thinking. Because I *was*.

Whatever book it was, I was *always* enjoying it. And since my family did not go to church on Sundays, Ms. Tomlin was right—I would see her tomorrow.

I rode my bike home, my Saturday routine, never quite sure what I'd find when I arrived, whether it would be my mom self-medicating with alcohol, my parents fighting.

Or worse.

I was always more fearful than I wanted to be.

Sharon, meanwhile, was always off with her friends, finding any excuse she could *not* to be home. I envied her. For both her age and her autonomy.

But when I was in books, feeling both lost and yet somehow found, I didn't have to fear anything. That day's checked-out library books were always lying in my bike's small basket, weighing it down, to be read that night and returned and replaced within the week, when Ms. Tomlin would have another recommendation or two waiting for me.

Books were my homebound escape, especially in the hot, schoolless months of summer.

***

As much as I enjoyed the freedom summer afforded me as a kid, as much as I'll *forever* enjoy the freedom books and libraries give me, it was winter that would forever have my child heart. The season promotes huddling by fires and familial closeness, two things my family simply didn't do any other time of the year. But come winter's frigid temperatures ... come snow and holiday decorations and hot apple cider ...

Those things and more brought a specific, annual joy into my world, a joy otherwise largely absent from my life.

"Carrie, it's time to go visit Santa!" my mom chirped. "Get ready!"

"Who's Santa?" I asked. It's the first memory I have of me in a "real" conversation. I might have been three ... maybe younger.

Who knew this question, in so many ways, would define my life from that point on? Certainly not maybe-three-year-old Carrie Clark.

My mom stood at my bedroom door, looking happy and ready for the day at ten in the morning, both rare for her. She'd also gotten dressed up. Whoever this Santa was, he mattered to Mom. Maybe more than Dad did. Dad, who was too busy working that weekend—and most weekends—to join his family.

"Who's Santa?! Oh, Carrie ... Santa is ... well..."

Watching my mom's body try to work in tandem with her brain to puzzle her way through this question of how exactly to explain to her little girl not just who but also *what* Santa Claus is ... was something I'd never forget, even though I didn't yet comprehend the why of it. Mom's halting, less-than-confident speech, so out of character for her, was the thing that donated this exchange to my memory to stay for good. Her facial muscles worked harder than her vocal chords for most of a long moment. And then she said:

"Santa's someone you'll love, Carrie."

"Do you love him?" I asked.

She didn't answer immediately before she replied, "Yes, I do, sweetheart."

"Why?" At three, the question I asked most often was why. Today, Dad always says I was forever asking why back then. I believe him because I've met my niece, Emily, and she does the same thing.

"I love Santa," Mom answered, "because Santa is magic. And magic is easy to love."

"I want to see the magic!" I said.

"Then you should hurry up and get dressed, sweet girl. Come on now. Your sister's already in the car waiting for us."

***

I'll always love *my* Santa. So will Mom. Whenever we approached his Santa-chair, Mom lit up like a firefly. I loved Santa because of how he lit up when he saw *me*.

Sure, other kids sat on his lap and asked him for toys, too. That's what happens at the mall every Christmas, Mom told me. But the twinkle in Santa's eye seemed a little different when he saw me. Or did every kid feel that way about their visits with *their* Santa?

My Santa remained *my Santa* throughout all my Santa years. From my first visit aged three to my last, just after I'd turned twelve, when I knew what I knew about Santa but didn't say anything because the last thing I wanted to mark *that* particular Christmas season was the breaking of my mother's heart.

The first year I *remember* asking my Santa for something, I was seven.

"And what's your name, sweetie?" Santa asked.

"I'm Carrie."

"I'm Santa," he said, and he ho-ho-hoed.

"I know," I answered with a laugh.

"It's the beard. Everybody knows. I can't go anywhere these days," Santa fake-lamented. "What would you like for Christmas, Ms. Carrie?"

"I want a big-girl bike. Can you do that, Santa?"

"It's very possible. The elves and I have been building bikes forever. I'll look into it when I get back to The North Pole."

Sharon had asked for makeup or something. She'd sat on Santa's lap that year because Mom told her to.

"Can't you do it for Carrie?" Mom had asked.

A perturbed Sharon gave an angry, exaggerated shrug. "For Carrie." That was the last year Sharon accompanied us to the mall to see Santa.

Seven-year-old Carrie loved riding her bike. More importantly, Santa had looked into it, the bike request (he might have even talked to Mom, for all I know), and then he'd delivered, as I'd hoped he would. I also knew how to read at seven. Not super well just yet, but well enough. *Thanks, Sharon.* Dad attached a basket to my new bike. "For all those books of yours," he said.

At nine, I didn't really want to visit Santa anymore. It wasn't cool. It wasn't something Sharon would do. Sharon, who'd just moved out of the house and gone off "to get smarter," as Dad put it. That I couldn't go with her was a travesty in itself. But Mom insisted we visit the mall as another Christmas approached, that we visit *my* Santa, who was quite obviously *her* Santa, too. She got all dressed up again. As ever. Her excitement was contagious. For Mom, I went. She made eyes at *my* Santa. Eyes I'd never seen her make at Dad. In truth, I hadn't even seen them embrace since I was four and a half.

***

By the time I was twelve, Dad had lived in a different house for almost a full year. He'd left *our* family home, the only one I'd known and the one he and Mom built together—with Sharon in tow before I came along and joined them. He packed everything he owned—which wasn't much, since most everything in the house was Mom's—into what was now a much older, less reliable Honda Accord. Mom drove her own car by this point.

As it turns out, that one cross-country trip in the Honda Dis-Accord when I was six was our last trip as a family to anywhere besides the grocery store. The big fight they'd had in our hotel suite on that trip, the first of many I witnessed, pretty much ensured this. I was in my own hotel bed, just feet from theirs, when Mom and Dad started up. I held my eyes shut tight, pretended to be asleep. They never suspected I heard any of it. But I heard it all. That's not to say I *understood* it all. I felt the anger, though.

"What the hell is wrong with you, James?" Mom started, her tone a quiet accusation.

"What do you mean?"

"It's like you're barely here anymore. Since Sharon's left home, you—"

"What do you want from me, Ruth?" said Dad. "I came on this trip, didn't I?"

"You wouldn't be here if it weren't for Carrie."

"*We* wouldn't be here if it weren't for Carrie. Come on, Ruth, admit it. You don't even like me anymore."

A long pause came next. For a moment, I thought my parents were done for the night, ready to sleep. I sure was, but as long as their fight went on, there would be no sleep. I peeked at them through one open eye. Mom was as far from Dad as she could get while still sharing their bed.

Then, through tears, Mom responded at last, "It's hard for me to like you, James, when I know you'd rather be with someone else."

***

Six years, and about a thousand fights later—too many of which I heard through thin walls—their content so repetitive I could say the lines before the players on that real-life stage, we prepared for Christmas at the Clarks. My twelfth and the first with Dad living somewhere else. Even so, that Christmas season was extra special to me because Sharon, now a junior in college at the University Of Washington, would be home to visit from Christmas Eve to January 4, when she would be expected back at school. Before she left for home, I called Sharon in her dorm.

I wanted to warn her, to make sure she understood the strain our family was under. The uncomfortable truth she'd be walking into.

Sharon answered her phone on the first ring, the second she saw it was me calling. "Hey, little sis! You ready for Christmas?"

"I guess."

"What do you mean, Carrie? You love Christmas."

I sat on my bed. My back against the wall, my body gently rocking back and forth. "I do. But it's weird over here."

"Since Dad left?"

35

"Since way before that, actually," I admitted. "But, yeah. Dad being gone ... it doesn't help."

"I figured. I knew Mom was having a hard time after I left. I don't think I realized how hard it's been for Dad. Guess I thought he'd just ... handle it, the way he always handles everything."

"How long has Dad been cheating on Mom?" A pointed question, sure, but I was convinced the only person who'd ever tell me the truth about this was my big sister Sharon.

"Dad *never* cheated on Mom."

"Never?"

I imagined Sharon shaking her head on the other end of the line. "He never would. But when Mom gets in her moods, she gets in her head, she gets suspicious, and she thinks he's cheating."

I exhaled deeply. *My dad is not cheating. He's not a cheater.* This family could still be saved, if ... "Sharon?"

"Yeah?"

"Do you think Mom and Dad still love each other?"

"I *know* they do," said my sister.

"How do you know?"

"I'll tell you when I get home, okay? I gotta get packed. I'll be there tomorrow, Carrie. Early. I can't wait to see all of you."

"But especially me, right?" I pressed.

She laughed. "But especially you," she repeated.

***

Our parents decided Dad would sleep at the original Clark house for Christmas. In the guest room. Mom's compromise, I knew. To make things easier on everyone, but at least for the holiday, our family would be together again.

Sharon wasn't joking—she did arrive early. Just before seven the next morning, December 23. After she'd spent about a half an hour unpacking, I pulled her into my room. I had to know.

"How do you know Mom and Dad still love each other?" *No ducking the question today, big sis,* I thought.

"I see it in the way they smile at each other."

"You mean *smiled?* When was that? Before I was born, obviously," I theorized, and then I grabbed onto Sharon. Sharon was tall even then. I hugged her waist.

"Carrie, life gets in the way. And this really isn't something *I* should be telling you. I should leave this to them. To Mom and Dad, I mean. It's their story." She paused like a pilot in a doomed aircraft in search of the eject button. "When are you going to see Santa?"

"Tomorrow. I can't believe Mom's making me go *again.* I'm twelve. I haven't been to see Santa in *three years.* When will I stop being her little baby?"

Now Sharon gave a genuine smile. "Short answer: never."

"Never?" *How depressing,* I thought.

"Do the Santa-bit for one more year. For Mom. I promise everything will make so much more sense tomorrow. In fact, I'll do what I can to make sure of it."

It is a testament to my love for my big sister that I didn't question this edict. I nodded, and she gave a short nod back, and the two of us made our way down to breakfast, Sharon in the same clothes she'd worn on the drive from the university and me still in my pajamas. I can say for sure what we wore not because I remember it exactly but because Mom took so many pictures that morning. Of our first breakfast as a full-fledged family in months.

Mom and Dad even smiled at each other once or twice. Though I doubted the smiles were earnest.

***

The next day, it was time for *my* Santa. *Mom's* Santa. *Our* Santa. I was sure she'd make eyes at the bearded man again this year. Dad, meanwhile, had to work, which surprised no one. Mom didn't even argue when he told us he'd be unable to accompany us to the mall.

"But *I'll* be there," Sharon put in, when the thought of Dad's absence made my face fall. How would Mom and Dad ever realize they loved each other again if Dad wouldn't even spend a weekend afternoon in the same room with us?

Dad left for work an hour before we left, as we sat and ate bacon and eggs, and Mom asked me what I'd be asking Santa for that year.

"I don't know," I said, dejected.

"Well, you better figure it out!" she said, her voice pure cheer. This was Mom, doing everything she could to buoy me up through a trying holiday.

Without Dad there, though, no go. I couldn't even *fake* excitement. This was simply something I had to do. A chore.

***

That said, *my* Santa was happy to see me.

"Ms. Carrie Clark!" he boomed.

"Hi," I said. I tried not to sound too down. It wasn't this mall-Santa's fault my family had disintegrated.

"How old are you this year?" asked my Santa.

"I'm twelve."

"I haven't seen you in a couple years, I think."

"Since I was nine."

"Ah, it's been three years, then."

"Yeah."

"Hm. And what, may I ask, has kept you away?"

Real life. Growing up. Two parents who pretty much hate each other. Am I missing anything?

"Life got in the way, I guess," I parroted Sharon, who stood with Mom nearby. Recognizing her words, my sister beamed for just long enough for only me to see it.

"Sorry to hear that," said Santa.

"Sorry to tell you that," I said. Slowly but steadily, my enthusiasm for this Santa visit improved as we talked.

"I do my best each year to make this experience special for everyone who sees me."

Good on this mall-Santa for not breaking character, I thought. *He deserves praise for that. Or at least something of an olive branch from me.*

"You're still my favorite Santa, though. And my mom... she's always so excited to come and see you."

Santa's eyes took on a glint then. A shine. He wasn't quite crying, but he wasn't far from it. What did I say?

"This might be the last year I come and see you, though. I mean, I'll be a teenager next year. Time to grow up."

"Is it now?" said Santa, swallowing hard. "Well, in that case, Ms. Carrie Clark, what can Santa get you this Christmas?"

I looked to Mom and Sharon. They weren't watching me anymore; now they stood in hushed conversation. I wouldn't know until later that day exactly what they were discussing.

"My parents just can't get along, Santa," I said.

"Is that so?" Santa replied.

"Dad tries, but my mom is ... well, she's a force of nature. There's no way around it. They've separated, and I get the feeling there's no way around that, either."

"I'm sorry to hear that, Carrie."

Santa did appear genuinely apologetic. *Why?* I wondered. *It's not his fault our family is broken.*

"So you want Santa to help your parents find love again? Well, unfortunately, Carrie, romantic love is a bit above Santa's pay grade, so I don't think—"

"No, that's not what I want," I interrupted.

"It's not?"

"My mom and dad aren't happy, Santa. To force them to live together and pretend love just for me ... that wouldn't be fair. But there is one thing I'll be wishing for until it happens."

"Ho-ho-ho, what's that, Carrie? What is Ms. Carrie Clark's Christmas wish?"

"I wish I could marry Santa Claus." My wish brought to Santa's face an expression I could not read.

"Not you, of course," I clarified. "Even though you're *my* Santa, I know you're just one of Santa's helpers. I'll be on the lookout for the *real* Santa. We'll go and live up at The North Pole. And we'll love each other in a way my parents never quite could love each other."

Now Santa took a handkerchief from his pocket and began dabbing at his eyes. I hopped down from his lap and gave my Santa one last hug.

"I'll always love you," I told him.

"And I you, little lady," he said and croaked out a halfhearted "ho-ho-ho."

***

"Did you have a good chat with Santa?" Mom asked when I returned to her and Sharon.

"I did."

"What did you ask him for?"

"Nothing really."

"Why not?" Mom's own face edged toward disappointment.

"I told him one of my wishes instead. I'm going to marry *the real Santa* and live at The North Pole with him. And we're never gonna fight the way you and dad fight. We're gonna ... do better."

Mom and Sharon shared a glance. Then Sharon said, "Hey, little sis ... why don't you come with me? The games at the arcade won't play themselves!"

I bounded after my big sister, grateful we'd have one more day of childhood together.

***

Once we'd left Mom's presence, when we were about halfway to the arcade, Sharon told me the truth.

"So you're gonna marry Santa, huh?" she started.

"Well, it's my wish, so I'm sure gonna try," I said, giving a weak smile.

"You know who else married Santa Claus, Carrie?" Just then, we reached the arcade, and Sharon took a small pouch from around her neck. A pouch, as it turned out, that she'd filled with quarters. "I usually use these for laundry," she said, dropping one into the first game we came to. "But since I'm home, I can spend them on something else this week!" She paused. "What was I saying before?"

"You were asking me who else married Santa. And I was about to say Mrs. Claus."

"Well, for sure Mrs. Claus did. But do you know who else married Santa?"

"Should I know?" I asked, clearly outside of some loop in which my mother and sister were firmly entrenched.

"The answer's Mom, Carrie," Sharon revealed.

"Mom?"

"Yeah. Mom married Santa, too. Why do you think she always wanted so badly to come visit him? Seeing *her* Santa—our Santa ... it reminded her why she fell for Dad in the first place."

"But they're *done*, Sharon. They're not getting back together. They shouldn't." I'd stopped button-mashing whatever game Sharon and I were playing, and she was taking full advantage. As she answered back, I watched my character die a gruesome, only-in-video-games death, as his heart came out his throat.

"No, they're not. And I think you're right, they shouldn't. But love is a funny thing, sis. People can grow apart, like Mom and Dad have. But we—you and me, Carrie—we are proof positive that, not so long ago, *our* Santa and *his* Mrs. Claus loved each other very much. So I hope you find *your* Santa, Carrie. Heck, I hope we both do."

I looked up at Sharon and smiled. "I will. One day I will. Obviously, he'll like Christmas. That's a given. I hope he likes storytelling as much as I do."

"He better," Sharon agreed. "Mom doesn't call you her little bookworm for nothing."

I giggled. "This bookworm will one day have her own real story to tell, I hope."

"You *hope* so?"

"Ah, who am I kidding? I know so! 'Til it comes true ... I'm gonna label it 'Carrie Clark's Christmas Wish.'"

Find out just how Carrie Clark's wish is fulfilled
in the novel

The Santa Claus Agreement.

–in hardcover, paperback, and e-book –

and *FREE* on Kindle Unlimited

(at certain times—check for availability)

Find out more about

The Santa Claus Agreement

in the **Also Available** section of this book

THE BELL-RINGER

For me, the best part of the hustle and bustle of the city is how anonymous I can be within it. How easily I'm able to blend in and get lost in a minute. And how I'm able to travel anywhere I want to go. As long as I have a purpose, I can go anyplace: traverse along any sidewalk, any street, or along any space. That's what they said. That's the one rule.

My purpose is my bell and the sound we make together. It's my signature sound—my only signature—as my favorite holiday draws near.

I am a bell-ringer.

My bell isn't a large church bell that peels more than it chimes. That, in equal measure—which, nonetheless, cannot be equal—celebrates weddings and laments demise. My bell isn't a doorbell or a now-all-but-obsolete telephone bell that both annoy more than they ring. Nor is it the school bell that calls its students back to class, the mere thought of it sobering.

No, mine is a bell of celebration!

Rejoice in its ringing, in its tiny, plaintive voice. Rejoice in just how my bell was my choice.

When asked what they wanted to do, some of my contemporaries desired to fly higher than airplanes ever flew. And so they did. Others wished to know an athlete's freedom. What it's like to blaze down a cinder track or to generate the ferocious crack of a baseball bat.

Not me.

The bell-ringer cheers at snow, at Christmas lights aglow. At family hunkering down, at a lost love found.

45

The bell-ringer cheers at simplicity. At how, here, no one will jeer at me.

Maybe I'll do something else sometime. Perhaps, I'll find another vocation I think just as fine. But, in this Christmas season, when thy will be done on Earth as it is in Heaven, I'll walk these streets—by the way, gold they are not—and, with my bell, broken spirits I'll leaven.

**

When I was a boy, not as long ago as you might think, and my mother would take me and my sisters to visit the big department store festooned with decorations and the Santa seated near its window and waiting to learn our childish wants and dreams, I was never as excited as my younger siblings.

Oh, I put on a good act for the girls, of course, but this time at the department store didn't affect me as it did them. But on our journey to the department store, I'd never fail to spot at least three different people ringing bells and kindly soliciting donations for the less fortunate, the downtrodden. They would post themselves on street corners and ring their bells in a metronomic motion, appropriately uniformed and costumed for the holiday.

I admired these people. Doing something worthy and good for humanity. And, though they'd pick a street corner and stay there for hours, ringing their bells like unthinking animatronics, I admired how they could move. They could go anywhere and they would be welcome there.

That's not how it is for a man living with a disability in a society only open enough to reveal (to those willing to see) just how closed it actually is. So, when I made it to Heaven and my comrades wanted to fly or to glide down a track with a sprinter's speed, I asked for my first job in this new place to be that of a bell-ringer, because from what I remembered, bell-ringers not only did good, they could also go anywhere and be accepted anywhere.

THE FAIRNESS OF LIFE

L ife wasn't fair.

At twenty-eight, his hair already thinning and graying with the stress of it, no one needed to convince Tim Harper of this. In fact, as far as he was concerned, his life *proved* the unfairness of all things about the human condition, proved it with the detailed research of a well-funded scientific study commissioned by the devil himself.

In his youth, Tim had found Melissa. A petite, oval-faced, blonde beauty. They met in high school science class, where he was her lab partner, and she was doing his science homework for him before *he* did her English homework for her in college. While applying for loans, they entered into the kind of partnership about which it is customary to first inform the government and then in celebration of which their families attended a small, enthusiastically thrown-together wedding.

It was small and enthusiastically thrown together because Tim and Melissa knew something no one else did: their two-person family would soon number three.

At that time, though they had no money, the little family—two, soon to be three—thought life not just fair but the kind of beautiful only Hollywood seemed able to touch. Tim and Melissa were brought up by people-who-loved-movies, brought up to love movies. And, more importantly, they cherished each other, making a point of adhering to Friday date-nights well into Melissa's third trimester. Only the doctor's insistence that Melissa go on bedrest put a stop to those public movie-nights, but inside their happy, modest home, the movie-nights went on.

***

Jamie Anne Harper, a little spitfire of a thing, came early by about a week. Which Melissa was glad for as there had been talk of a C-section if the baby dawdled, and she did not want that. She was glad the pregnancy would not end in a long scar.

"Thanks for coming, little one," Melissa said as the baby—spent from her journey—slept, content at last, on her chest. "We're gonna have fun, you and me. I've always wanted a little girl. We're gonna be best friends."

Then she offered Jaime to Tim. "Here, Dad."

***

When Tim thought back on it, to determine the exact instant when life had turned cold on him, when the truth of the unfairness of life began to rule his respirations—which would not stop, as much as he wanted them to—he came back to Christmas. Even though some would claim it had to have happened earlier, that he was living in a world clouded by recency bias, he wouldn't hear of it.

Jamie's eighth Christmas.

Melissa, always willing to help a friend in need, had gone to help a just-divorced, just-moved friend dig around and find enough of the former family's holiday decorations to cobble together a Christmas for two children whose home was now and forever broken.

Tim remembered, with a clarity he detested, Melissa saying into the phone, "Oh, you have a place! That's wonderful, Sal. So why are you crying? This is a happy day, isn't it?"

He'd looked over to see Melissa writing something down as she held the phone to her ear. An address, he guessed. Then she said, "Well, *no* time is ideal for this sort of thing. You had to leave. Had to. You were doing what was right for you and your boys, Sal."

God, she used that nickname a lot. Sal. Sally. After that night, Tim would not speak to the woman Melissa called Sal. Not ever again, he promised himself. Not because she'd done anything wrong. She hadn't. But Tim saw Sal as the reason he got a call later that night from a concerned-sounding police officer ...

Melissa should have been home an hour or so ago, if this had been a normal night of Melissa-helps-a-down-on-their-luck-friend.

Instead, he had to go down to the morgue to identify his beloved wife as the victim of a drunk driver's hubris.

Tim Harper became a single father in the blink of an eye. Forget speaking to her; Tim hadn't even *looked* at Sally as she sat, inconsolable, in a church pew, all by herself at Melissa's too-early funeral.

We should have had fifty years, Tim lamented.

When Sally approached him to apologize, though neither of them knew for what, Tim couldn't hear it and so, before Sally could say it, he acted as though he saw someone approaching he just *had* to talk to. Right then. *Anyone but her*, Melissa's former best friend. Sally the divorcee, who'd made him a widower left to raise an eight-year-old girl.

Tim didn't know the first thing about braiding hair.

Life, as it turned out, wasn't fair in the least.

***

Then Jamie broke her leg.

It was a week before Christmas. Melissa had only been gone two weeks. The funeral was still too fresh in the minds of its attendees, and too many casserole dishes still sat in a too-small-for-them fridge. Tim was grateful not to have to cook for both he and Jamie when he came home from work each day, wrung out and silently seething. He was grateful and he wasn't, all at the same time.

If Melissa were here, he thought, *those damn casserole dishes wouldn't be.* Tim would have made that trade. His wife and the fifty years they'd promised each other, in sickness and in health, for four battered casserole dishes, returned post-haste, to the kitchens from whence they'd come. But since no one was offering such a swap, he could only make that trade in his dreams, and so he tried to lose himself in them.

And he would have, if it weren't for Jamie and how the little girl needed him.

***

"Mr. Harper, I'm Officer Samuels of the Seattle Police Department."

Seated at work and looking out his office window, Tim saw a view of precisely nothing. His head swam. His guts whirled. He wished he hadn't eaten lunch.

"Where is she?" was all he could manage after he'd been told, precisely and formally, about the accident.

Melissa had been gone before he could ask this question. On some level, he was grateful he could ask it now, about Jamie. Then he was angry at himself for being grateful.

"Your daughter has been taken to the hospital by ambulance, sir. She was conscious when responders arrived. She was able to tell them her name, who you are, all the important stuff, but soon after, she lapsed into unconsciousness. Sir, you need to get here as soon as you can."

He left work with a clipped explanation of, "Emergency!" to his colleagues.

No one questioned him. They thought life unfair to the man, and they stayed clear of poor Tim Harper, didn't even touch him, so as not to allow his bad luck to somehow become theirs.

***

He was asleep at Jamie's bedside—was it that night or the next? He wasn't sure—when a nurse walked into Jamie's room, which woke him. He straightened in his seat, trying to appear as though he'd been awake for more than five seconds. She picked up the little girl's chart and gave it a glance.

"You must be Dad," she said.

"Tim Harper," he said reflexively, shaking her hand. His grip wasn't tight enough, and Tim's own father would have admonished him for this, but he didn't care. Some things mattered, and some things didn't. His little girl was knocking at Death's door, to see if the specter were home. *That* mattered. Death was one hand Tim refused to shake, and he hoped Jaime felt the same.

"You have a strong little girl there, Mr. Harper, let me tell you."

"Can you tell me again how this happened?" Tim was pretty sure a doctor had happened by with the particulars hours ago, but he'd been asleep or in a stupor or some combination of the two. He remembered none of it.

"Jamie was riding her bike ..."

That's why he'd heard none of it. Because they'd started with how Jamie was riding her bike, and this made him think of Melissa. How teaching their daughter to ride her bike had been the last thing Melissa had done before the *actual* last thing she'd done, helping to arrange Sal's life even as hers had nothing left in it to arrange.

Tim fought to listen. His fight-or-flight reflex lobbied to carry him away as it had once before, but he fought to hear the words.

"Jamie was turning for home, I was told, when a kid ran a red light ..."

"A kid?"

The nurse wore sympathy. "The paramedics who brought her in said the kid had just gotten his learner's permit. He was driving with his mother. He'd hit the gas instead of the brake. They don't think he ran the light; they think he was trying to stop. He just ..."

The nurse didn't say it. She didn't need to. The kid had gotten confused. Gas or brake? Brake or gas? Which is which?

***

Tim liked the nurse, whose name was Esther. She was a sturdy, brown-haired, no-nonsense, I'm-here-to-help lady, and that's what his daughter needed right now. Hell, that was what they *both* needed right now.

Esther worked the graveyard shift. She'd talk to him late at night when visiting hours were over, when he should technically have been removed and told to go home, get some rest in his own bed, and return in the morning. Most nurses would have removed him like this. Esther did not.

"Tell me about your little girl," Esther said to him. She was looking over Jamie's chart again.

"She's ... my life." Tim found himself being the kind of honest he didn't like being. Honest meant vulnerable. The last person he'd been vulnerable like that with ... was a week in the ground.

"That's beautiful," Esther said.

"Is it?"

"It is." Her tone was far too cheery.

"Her mama is gone," Tim said. Why was he sharing this? It must have something to do with the vulnerability. That was all he knew.

"No."

"Yes."

"That's awful."

"It is."

"And right before Christmas."

"Yep. It doesn't matter when. It just hurts ... hurts like hell anytime. All the time."

"Of course," Esther agreed.

Tim expected Esther to ask how it had happened, his wife's demise. Everyone who learned of her passing would ask this. As though it was *the thing* to ask. Esther didn't.

Thank Christ.

"Time to pick yourself up, huh?" Esther said.

"What do you mean?"

"For your little girl. For Jamie."

"If she wakes up."

"She'll wake up, Dad." Esther sounded sure of herself, and it threw Tim a moment.

"She will?"

Esther nodded.

"How do you know?"

Esther pointed at her nametag, at her uniform. "Nurse," she said. That was all.

"I loved her mother, you know. And she loved me. We met in high school and went to college together. In the middle of slogging through college, we got pregnant with Jamie."

"What a blessing!" Esther said in an excited-but-it's-nighttime-and-I-can't-be-too-loud whisper.

"We thought so. We loved each other so much. People said we were made for each other. My mother was always saying that. But then ..."

"Life changed things."

"Changed them in a blink."

"Life will do that." She came over to adjust the IV above Jamie's bed. "So what are you gonna do?"

Tim thought of all the Christmas presents that sat in his bedroom closet. He hadn't had it in his heart to put up a tree yet. Not that Jamie would let him. That was a with-Mommy activity, she said.

All but a couple of those gifts in the closet were for his daughter: toys she'd wanted with a passion that Tim had thought would be reserved for a teenage girl's first boy band, and a couple books Melissa had said Jamie was old enough to begin reading now. The Phantom Tollbooth was one of them. Their daughter would be a reader, his wife had insisted, and Tim knew better than to argue.

"We're gonna ... do Christmas, I guess. Can't say I'm excited about it. I don't think she'll be, either. When she wakes up." He looked at his daughter's diminished form, half-hidden beneath the sheets of her hospital bed. "I'll need to get a tree."

"I like that," Esther said.

"What do you like?"

"You said 'when she wakes up.' That's faith, Dad. Good for you."

"Even if I have faith she'll wake up, even if I can manage to find that faith somewhere, her mama is gone for good. We can't get her back."

"Maybe you're not supposed to."

Tim sat straight up in his seat, offended. "Excuse me?"

"Faith isn't blind, Dad. Some people may think it is, but it's a lot more complicated than that. When life is unfair, it isn't being unfair to you just for the sake of being unfair to you personally. When it's unfair to you, it's evening the ledger with someone else. You just can't often see the ledger getting evened out because you're not looking for it. And why should you be looking for it?"

"I refuse to believe my wife's passing made life better for someone. For anyone!" he said.

"That isn't what I'm saying. You're overtired, Dad. You should get some rest. Your little girl will be awake in the morning, and she's going to need you."

Tim wanted to argue some more, and he would have, but his energy was sapped. Gone to nothing, so he simply did as Esther suggested.

He slept. In fact, for the first time in a month, he slept deeply.

***

Jamie woke as Esther said she would. And it was Jamie who woke her father.

"Dad ...?"

He didn't move.

"Dad!"

Now he startled, awake.

"What ... Melissa, what?" Tim had been dreaming of his wife.

"It's Jamie, Dad."

He wiped his eyes, all the while willing the last image of the dream—one of Melissa's lips about to meet his—to stay with him. Even as the image fled with the daylight, he willed it to stay, but his will was not strong enough, and it was gone, too.

"When are we going home, Dad?"

"What ...? Jaime ...? Jaime!" It took a moment for him to process the voice of his daughter, after days of a silence so loud he could hear it. "Home... yes. When the doctors say we can, honey, that's when."

"I miss Mom," Jamie said, and Tim knew Jaime was back and that she would not be leaving, so he needed to come back to life too.

"I do too, honey. I do too."

***

Jamie's return to consciousness wasn't a miracle, the doctors explained. Not exactly. But it was far from the norm, and it had the medical professionals a tad perplexed.

"Check her chart," Tim told one of them. ... Doctor Jones, his nametag announced. "The nurse on the graveyard shift came by yesterday, and she's always checking her chart, and yesterday she told me Jamie would wake up this morning. And ... well ... look."

"I'm awake!" Jamie confirmed.

"So you are," said Dr. Jones. "Mr. Harper, may I see you in the hall for a moment?"

***

In the hall, Dr. Jones asked, "You are aware that visiting hours in this hospital end at 8 p.m., are you not, Mr. Harper?"

"I am," said Tim.

"Then, with all due respect sir, what were you doing here over the *graveyard* shift?"

"That's my daughter in there, Doctor, and she's been asleep up until this morning, and ... well, I wasn't leaving, and Nurse Esther doesn't seem the type to make grieving men leave the hospital when they don't *want* to leave the hospital."

Doctor Jones furrowed his brow. "Nurse ... what was that name again?"

"Esther. Nurse Esther."

The doctor cleared his throat, took a step towards Tim. "Sir, I've worked in this hospital thirty years. As long as I've worked here, Mr. Harper, we have never had a nurse here by the name of Esther."

***

Tim Harper drove his daughter home that day, after she'd been fitted with a cast her friends would spend all winter signing in all manner of pen ink. Blues and reds and oranges and yellows and some colors Tim wouldn't even be able to name. He drove home in a state that went beyond confusion.

As long as I've worked here, Mr. Harper... we have never had a nurse here by the name of Esther.

When they made it home, Tim and Jamie Harper found three people waiting in their driveway: Melissa's friend Sally and her two boys, Logan and Blake, who jumped down from Sally's minivan.

"Mr. Harper! Jamie!" Logan called. "We got you a tree!"

Logan was only a few years older than Jamie, Blake a few years her junior.

"That was supposed to be a surprise," Sally scolded lightly.

"There's a tree on our car. What's surprising about that? Everyone can see it, Mom."

Tim approached Sally, and the fury he'd felt for her since Melissa's loss returned in full. "Sally, you should have called first. We're just getting home. Jamie is tired, and I ..."

"I'm not tired, Dad," Jamie said, undercutting him.

He wanted to scream ... not at his daughter, not even at the object of his fury. He just wanted to scream. But he wouldn't.

Sally spoke, soft and slow. "Tim, I know you hate me. I know I'm the last person you want to see right now."

On this, at least, they could agree.

"I've been blaming myself ever since Melissa ... well, you know, ever since it happened. And there's absolutely nothing I can do to make it right. Your wife is gone ...

Jamie's mom is gone. My best friend is ... I understand why you haven't spoken to me, Tim. I tried to see Jamie at the hospital, but they said you weren't allowing visitors, so I ..."

"She's been out cold until today," Tim offered.

"Right. Well ... anyway, Logan kinda spoiled the surprise, but we got you a tree. Figured you needed that more than you needed another casserole."

He nodded.

"And I checked your mail."

"You what?"

"I didn't *open* it. Melissa gave me a mailbox key in case of emergencies, and I figured this had to be an emergency. So here you go."

With that, Sally handed him a pile of mail significantly smaller than he'd expected. Obviously, she'd culled out the junk mail and tossed it out in the same way Melissa would have done. What remained were three pieces of mail. One from the funeral home. It choked him up all over again. He'd get to the bills and the business of life later. And there was one from his mother—a Christmas card for Jamie, he guessed, based on the red and green envelope with the Santa stamp affixed to it.

Then there was an envelope that had no postage on it, which made Tim wonder how it had managed to get to where it needed to go. His mailbox, obviously, addressed to Tim & Jamie Harper. In the area of the return address, two simple words told Tim who the letter had come from: Nurse Esther.

***

You've probably figured it out by now, Dad. That I shouldn't have been where I was when you were where I was. The laws of the universe would usually forbid such a thing. We're not permitted to directly affect our own.

Once, not so long ago, I was human, just like you, and I was lucky. I got the chance to live a full life, find love, raise a family, all the things you'd want in a life. The things I know you wanted, and still want.

In life, I was a nurse, though, as the good Doctor Jones knows, not at the hospital where your Jamie was. When I passed and shifted into this "afterlife," I was given a choice: merge onto a new plane in this new place or exist in a new form, and in this existence I would guard and protect others. I was, after all, qualified, in a way.

I chose to be what you call an angel. Time works differently for us here, and you and Jaime are the one hundredth case I've attended. Every soul I help is special, yet this case in particular is special to me. I get to help five people, not just one or two.

You were very much self-focused when we met, Dad. I understand why. It felt like your life was cratering. I wouldn't have expected you to act any other way. But since you were as self-focused as you were, you never asked about me. But then, why should you have? But I can tell you what I need to now. I will tell you, because I'm asking you to help me.

I had a granddaughter, whom I loved ... whom I love very much. She has two young boys, and she had to find the courage to remove them and herself from an abusive situation. I am so proud of her. I always called her Sal, which is why her best friend always called her Sal. Her best friend, I know, was your wife, Melissa, and we communed, she and I. In our new existence, we communed.

I know this is a lot to take in, Dad. So don't take it all in. Not right now. At this moment, you need to celebrate Christmas with your daughter. And so here is what I ask: please find it in your heart to include my granddaughter, my Sal, and her boys in your celebration. Let's say that two of us are asking this of you.

Two families need not—should not—be alone at Christmas. "The rest," as they say, will take care of itself.

Have faith, Dad.

Merry Christmas,

Nurse Esther

Derek McFadden

WRITTEN BY THE VICTORS:
A VIGNETTE

On what would become, perhaps oddly, my favorite Christmas, my grandpa wasn't well. He hadn't been well for years, but his decline was noticeable now in a way it hadn't been before. Or maybe we'd just been purposefully looking the other way, not wanting the truth to show itself to us.

The truth was that my papa's cancer was winning, against both lungs, its pyrrhic victory soon to come, *too soon*, even though he said he was fine and that going bald from the chemo didn't bother him. And it didn't, Grandma agreed. Not as much as it bothered him that those chemo drugs wouldn't let him lie out in summer's inviting afternoon sun.

When winter came, something akin to relief came over him. He didn't have to go outside, and he wasn't expected to amble out of the house in his diminished form. He could just be who he was to us.

It didn't matter that his Santa was now the skinniest Santa I'd ever seen. It didn't matter that I was fifteen. I didn't sit on his lap, of course, but that Christmas I did tell him what I wanted for Christmas, what I wanted for the rest of my life.

We sat in his living room in a big blue three-person rocker. My papa, my brother, Ben, and me.

"I want to be a writer, Pop," I told him.

It didn't really need to be said. He knew. Papa was already my first reader. He was no writer, but he *was* an avid reader, and he saw the promise in my work before I did. He was always asking me for "pages," and whenever he read a story he gave me notes—spotting plot holes, misplaced words, and dangling participles—and I listened to this man who'd fought—and seen his friends die—in Korea. I made his suggested changes with little argument, as though he weren't a former short-order cook and railroad switchman but an editor at one of the big New York publishing houses. *If only*, I thought, more than once. On the rare—and I mean *rare*—occasion when he told me a story was perfect and didn't need a thing done to it, I would perceive this piece as a singular snowflake, one I refused to mar with my oft-forced verbosity.

"You *are* a writer," Pop tried to assure me. "Just like Ben's an actor, you're a writer, Derek. Don't let anyone ever tell you different." His voice was reedy, but it still held the authority I'd known all my life.

Sure, I knew Ben was an actor. He was in plays. My dad bought him flowers for every one of his opening nights. And there were so many. Even back then, aged eleven, he went on commercial auditions, and I admired how Ben could slip into the skin of someone else.

With my cerebral palsy, I could *never* do that, never effortlessly become someone I wasn't and would never be. People clamored for what my brother did; they humored me. At least, that's how I saw it until Papa set his sights, aiming to set me straight.

"History is written by the victors, you know," Papa said that Christmas, all three of us holding cups of eggnog, although his cup of eggnog likely held something more in it because, "I'm dying soon, anyway. What the hell does it matter if I have a little something extra in my cup?"

What the hell did it matter.

"Who said that, Pop?" I asked. "That history is written by the victors?"

"Don't know." He shook his hairless head. "Whoever it was, though, they were right; it *is* written by the victors."

There was something in that phrase, something Papa wanted me to hear that I wasn't getting. I think that's why he repeated it. I looked at Ben to see if he understood. His face was blank, though, so I wasn't alone in my lack of comprehension. Good.

Papa wore a far-off look as he gazed at the last Christmas tree he'd ever see. I silently wondered if it was the most beautiful tree, or if that honor belonged to a conifer from his childhood so long ago.

"Did I do good?" he asked, taking a small sip of his nog.

"What do you mean, Pop?" I said.

Ben gave him a wordless glance of concern.

"Was I a good papa to you kids?"

"The best," Ben and I both said at the same time.

This brought a sad smile to his lips. "This cancer's gonna beat me, and it's gonna beat me soon. I know it. I'm not giving up—your grandmother would kill me herself if I gave up—but I know it."

Somewhere not far away, Grandma was singing a Christmas carol as only she could, so badly and too loudly, into the Christmas ether, but within hours, their house would be noisy with company that we only saw once a year, with food and the thankful saying of grace, and with games and present-openings. Grandma was getting the house ready with her last-minute decorating. There were so many Christmas lights around the house that the old fuses routinely blew out; she'd go down to their basement to change them.

Grandma might have been trying to make Ben and me laugh with her bad singing, but, after years of practice, my brother and I tuned her out as we listened to Papa.

"I want to stay, but ... ah, Christ," he said, "I can't. I want to see you both graduate high school and get married but ... I won't. That's why I need you guys to remember that history is written by the victors."

"I'm sorry, Pop, I don't—"

"*We* don't," corrected my brother.

"We don't understand what you're—"

"If you can write my story, Derek, if Ben can act my story ... well, then ... I won't have lost, will I?"

"Lost? What do you mean *lost?*" Looking at him, I fought to see through tears. I'd see this same clouded view in countless dreams for countless years going forward.

Pop looked at the both of us. "My actor," he said to Ben, who offered him a weak smile. Then he turned to me. "And my writer. Tell my story ..."

My grandfather was just about to turn eleven on a December Sunday when a surprise attack on Pearl Harbor shocked the nation into action it had no choice but to take. Which meant that, by the time my grandpa got to Korea in the 1950s—by the time he was drafted to Korea, where Uncle Sam charged him with both keeping communism at bay and keeping himself alive—the soldiers in his unit jokingly called their corporal radioman "old-timer" since he had close to a decade on some of them.

"I'd never been so scared in all my life," he'd once told my older cousins and Ben and me. He also told us an appendectomy scar he'd had since he was a boy was really a bayonet wound. We were young and impressionable, and we believed him because it sounded cool, despite the fact that no bayonet would ever go in at *that* angle. But his scar was cool. Which, he assured us, war was not.

"It's not like they make it look in the movies. People I knew died. They went with me to Korea, but they never made it home and lived their lives. Not like me."

He never talked about the survivor's guilt I knew he felt, though it was implied around his house. If I ever used the term "forgive and forget," Papa would stop me on the spot—wherever we were—and say, "You can forgive; you don't *ever* forget."

And he never had. Not through his years as a cook, a switchman, a family man. All those years he'd lived a life of giving and sharing of himself...

"Show everyone how I *fought to live*. Back then, now ... Tell them how, when I got home from the war, I helped make a home for your dad and your uncle. And then your grandma and I ... well, we just loved being grandparents to your cousins and to you kids. Made us feel young again. Every time I'd see one of Ben's plays, or read one of your stories, Derek, I'd think, Well, hell, look what these kids know. Look what they can do!

"As long as you two remember me, as long as you write or act or create with the memory of me by your side, I won't really have died. I'll still be living. Cancer be damned."

He cleared his throat.

"Speaking of your writing, you wouldn't happen to have any pages for me, would you, Derek? You should show me your newest story before the noisy ones get here

69

and this place turns into a madhouse and we're all bouncing off the walls!" Papa's eyes twinkled.

The thing none of us said, because to admit it meant defeat: Papa would be in his bedroom, fast asleep, in half an hour; his "cancer curfew." For the first and only time, he would not cook our family's Christmas dinner. He and Grandma would open their Christmas presents later, with no one watching, breaking our family tradition. How we'd watch intently as everyone else opened their presents. First the youngest among us, followed by the oldest, alternating like that for hours. Tradition. Sometimes it felt like it could take forever. But not this year.

Before all that, though, I did hand Papa my latest work, which I'd had at the ready, hoping he'd ask to see it. When he'd finished the read, he told me to trim twenty pages down to fifteen or less (always preferably less, "because less is more, Derek") and how I might increase the story's tension.

"Nothing happens until page three. You can do better than that."

I could, and we both knew it. Ben knew it, too, nodding along, having read the thing over Papa's shoulder.

***

On my favorite—my papa's last—Christmas, my grandfather made me a writer. His writer. Just as Ben was his actor. And as long as I live, and as long as my brother lives, and however many Christmases we spend on Earth, so will our papa. After all, history is written by the victors; cancer be damned.

Merry Christmas.

Listen to the audio version of *Written by the Victors*, narrated by the award-winning narrator BJ Harrison.

And it's FREE ...

Well, sort of!

We're asking for a $10 donation to **St. Jude Children's Research Hospital**.

www.bit.ly/victorsbyderek

After all, Christmas is for the children—*all* the children :).

WHO WE'LL BE

This year, the holidays were deeply dour. Who had ever celebrated Christmas over a computer before? Far-flung diplomats or soldiers readying for fights sanctioned by far-flung diplomats, sure; or the negotiators trying their best in the coldest months to keep nations free of hot squabbles that could turn into more, if men weren't careful. But who else?

Grace sat back in her chair and sighed. Was it really December 25th already? How could it be? It was just March yesterday, and everyone was going to movies and out to restaurants and visiting with other people *in person* in public. Before they were lawfully ordered to do nothing in the interest of public safety and shut up in the too-present solitude of their homes, their boxes full of alone, for a day that lasted nine months, a day that was ongoing and to which there appeared no end.

Christmas: the McCoy family's long-ago avowed and undisputed favorite holiday. Although Grace couldn't say whether it was she or her late husband, Ray, or one of the kids who'd first avowed it.

Were they really celebrating Christmas over something called Zome?

What the heck is this Zome thing, anyway? the frazzled older woman thought. She fixed her hair as best she could in the faint reflection of the screen in front of her. The woman who looked back at her was ... old. No other way to put it. No, she wasn't *that* old, was she? She liked to believe she wasn't. The people on her screen, none of whom she'd heard speak yet, evidenced otherwise, however. Almost all of them called her "Mom." Some went as far as "Grandma."

Well, she was a grandma. And she had been for some years. Three times over, in fact!

"Why is there an echo?" Grace asked, not expecting anyone to answer her. No one did. She tapped at her keyboard in an attempt to increase the computer's volume. "Hello, hello, hello?" It worked too well, in that she managed to increase the echo. "Is anyone else getting an echo, or is that just me? Is that supposed to happen ...? I ... I don't think that's supposed to happen, is it?"

Of the three people on her screen, she watched her two sons most intently. Her adult sons ... they were still kids to her and would always be kids to her. They'd always thought that was weird, but now that Greg and his sister Ally—his tardy sister (where was she?? Why wasn't she here yet?)—had kids of their own, they were beginning to understand.

Greg and Peter—and only God knew where Ally was— were in different rooms, of course. Each in a different city. Peter, her youngest at twenty-two, was even stuck in a different country. Costa Rica, to be precise. He'd gone because he was still in his twenties and *could* go, and a vacation and time away from the stresses of the everyday had sounded good to him. Relaxing. Needed.

The trip had been good to him, too. She could still make out the last vestiges of his vacation tan. It had been good, that vacation, until all goodness left the world without so much as a "Dear John letter." *More like a "Dear the World" letter*, thought Grace.

It was the virus, of course, that had changed everything. For all of them and for everyone else, but most immediately for Peter because the virus left him stranded.

This isn't how Christmas is supposed to go.

The plan—the it-never-changes-which-is-exactly-what-makes-it-a-great-plan plan—every year hardly ever varied, becoming A McCoy family tradition for fifteen Christmases now. (Did fifteen Christmases make for a tradition? Who was the arbiter for decisions like that? Was there such an entity, such a person, such a job?) Every year, Grace would bake her famous chocolate chip cookies with the help of one Ms. Georgia Grace and buy too much egg nog, and her family—kids and now *teenage* grandkids, God help her—would be there, as they were always there, and they'd sleep in their old rooms with their new families (though some members weren't all that new), and it would be as if they'd never left and yet as if they'd been gone forever. The nest would be full again, if only for one holiday each year. Minus her Ray, but "even the luckiest people in the universe can't have everything," as Ray himself had told her so many times.

She could hear it in his voice even five years after he'd gone.

It was two holidays, actually, so sayeth tradition, because her family stayed 'til after New Year's. But since both holidays took place within a week, it was all one lovely, unmissable period of time for a woman who now missed having her family at home, the kids to get ready for school, the PTA meetings to lead, a handsome husband she'd wake before work with fresh coffee and a kiss.

In more recent times, her family had shrunk to grandkids she now saw once a month, if she was lucky, when one of them—usually fifteen-year-old Georgia Grace, who seemed to be the only grandkid who didn't mind the task—got roped into Facetiming her for ten minutes to check and make sure Grandma was still breathing over there at the original Camp McCoy.

Grace McCoy sat now at her ancient computer, both relics of a bygone age, an age that had left Grace far behind. Crueler still, the era in which Grace McCoy had thrived—if there indeed were such an era once—had unceremoniously pulled up stakes one day and left town while she was sleepwalking through her life. It never told Grace it was going anywhere, nor how she might follow, and she woke one gray morning to an empty right side of a king-sized bed, to kids who didn't need her anymore, to grandkids who didn't understand her (seemingly ever), to a society sick with the blight of isolation masquerading as curated connection, and—lastly and worst of all—to some awful, unknowable virus taking aim at everyone without impunity.

On screen now, Greg, her eldest, sat in his home office, which was where he conducted all his meetings these days. Christmas, for him, had been reduced to just another meeting to get through, Grace realized with a level of sadness that struck her hard. To be conducted, completed, catalogued. Behind Greg, there was the usual smattering of mementos that marked him as a loving father; pictures were pinned, drawn by her namesake, Georgia Grace. She was still quite the avid would-be artist. That thought, at least, made Grace smile.

"I love that middle name of yours," Grace would say every visit whenever she first saw the little girl.

"My whowe name makes me sound wike I'm fwum da souf," said Georgia once when she was still somewhere in the single digits and her "r"s and "l"s were still both "w"s and "f"s. Grace had stifled a laugh, and she remembered hoping to herself that it would take any speech therapist years to correct the impediment. She'd always made sure to hide her smile because how she spoke and how she reacted made the little girl, an open heart too susceptible to the cruelty of the world—as all proper artists were— "sewf-conshus."

Damn all adults for ever making children like Georgia self-conscious about anything. For making true artists doubt their purpose. Wasn't life hard enough?

"Nice to see you, Mom." Greg's voice came through loud and clear now, no echo. Greg, with his close-cropped black hair and intense brown eyes, was so stiff. Had he always been that stiff? Was that the Zome and were they all a little uncomfortable? Or was Greg just uncomfortable around them? Uncomfortable talking to her? Did it have to do with his place in the family? As the eldest, Greg was set to become the executor of her estate, and he'd known this since before Ray had gone.

Grace had a goal this Christmas: she would cut through the small talk that, in the course of a normal holiday season, ruled and nearly ruined their first couple of days together. Lots of *hi moms* and *I'm fines* and *work's fine,* followed by everybody and their families retreating to their rooms and keeping to themselves until dinner or presents or when Grace's nightly family meetings insisted on their presence. The McCoys wouldn't do that this year, not least because those holidays all started with little white lies Grace didn't have the patience for this December.

Time to engage, she decided. *They're here. They're talking to you. It's Christmas. Seize this opportunity; it's an opportunity so many might be jealous of today.*

"Merry Christmas, Greg, Peter, Ally …" By then, a little window with Ally's name in it had appeared, but there was still no sound, and it was black because she hadn't yet turned on her camera, but if she was there, then Grace would acknowledge her daughter. "And good morning and merry Christmas, Miss Georgia Grace. Sorry, but you know how I love that name. Merry Christmas, everyone!"

"Morning, Grandma. Merry Christmas!" Georgia—the only one to answer right away—beamed. Grace appreciated how different the teenager was from her father. Her mother's influence, surely.

"How's your mom, sweetie?" Grace asked her granddaughter.

"She called last night," Georgia said flatly, her smile gone quicker than Santa's sleigh after a delivery.

Grace nodded. The free-spirited Sue had left the family not long after Georgia was born, which accounted for why Grace so fiercely loved her only granddaughter.

For Georgia, Grace knew, this kind-of family togetherness today was a chance to connect with her loved ones she hadn't seen in months. A chance to smile and virtually hug people, like her Uncle Peter, whom she hadn't even *heard from* in about a month.

She's got all my best qualities. This thought reworked the wattage of Grace's smile. *How old is she now? Fifteen? A granddaughter of mine is* fifteen*? Oh, Lord. But I wasn't as engaged as Georgia at her age. If I had to do this at fifteen, I'd be bored to death and maybe bored beyond it.* At this silent turn of phrase, Grace cringed a little and caught herself. *We're all still alive.*

If there was to be a Christmas miracle this year, this had to be it. The tenuous and invisible strands that reached all the way down from Heaven and connected the McCoys were still, almost inexplicably, intact.

Grace paused and took a breath. *Georgia Grace. Focus on her. If you start thinking too hard about how lucky we all are to be here, it'll be all you think about today.*

Ray would want the family to live on. He'd taught them how to do it so that they'd come through the toughest times life had to offer unscathed. Or, if scathing could not be avoided, at least the McCoys might learn something from it.

Georgia. Talk to Georgia. Her granddaughter wore the same plaid flannel Christmas pajamas she'd have been wearing had she spent Christmas Eve at the family home making cookies with her grandmother. Grace was glad to see they'd arrived on time. She knew Georgia had been instructed, "Wear those pajamas to bed so Grandma can see you in them in the morning." At fifteen, though, Georgia likely frowned at the light edict, which doubtless came from her father, Greg. The teen, though, still played the role of dutiful daughter and granddaughter with nary a misstep. And there would be none now as she sat up in bed in her room, her hair tousled.

"Georgia, when did we talk last?" Grace asked.

Georgia thought a moment, her head lolling skyward toward a ceiling Grace couldn't see. "Not sure. Dad's birthday, maybe?"

Greg sat in his office, offering no confirmation. He was far more taciturn than his father—whom he took after in appearance—ever was. Far more conservative than his brother and sister. Grace and Ray would joke between themselves that Greg barely whimpered on appearing at his late-February birth, on time and ready to get on with this life thing, which should have been a sign of the man to come.

"It's a shock he didn't come out of my womb wearing an expensive business suit," Grace would quip. The kind her Ray would never buy. The kind Peter wouldn't wear unless he'd been kidnapped in the dead of night and his captors demanded he bow down to the Brooks Brothers.

Georgia was right. Her father's latest birthday "party" was held a week before silent night, a phrase that was no longer simply a hymn but now also aptly described life as a whole. That was the last time they'd seen each other.

Ally had been born next, two years after Greg. Grace's little firecracker of a redhead, Ally shared so many traits with her niece, Georgia. Both were kind but outspoken; neither suffered fools lightly, which, Grace mused, meant neither suffered Greg lightly. No one ever said Greg McCoy was a fool; he opened his mouth and said so for them. Ally's kids, Raymond, who was named after his grandfather, and Wesley, after his other grandfather, were at their father's, where they lived now. A decision arrived at a year ago after Ally's rules were deemed by the boys to be too strict and her ex-husband, Denny, promised his rules would "make sense." She hadn't seen them in person since March. No one would mention this today in Ally's virtual presence, but they all knew it, and they sympathized with her.

The most Greg would do to show sympathy was to give a wordless grunt (of support, Grace hoped.)

A new face popped up. *There* was her Ally! At last.

Georgia lit up at the sight of her aunt. Grace silently rejoiced. *All three of my kids. Right here. Right now.*

Well, sort of.

"Hey, Aunt Al." Georgia used the east coast pronunciation of the word aunt, in which the "u" was emphasized. As one who'd always used the west coast variant, which threw the "u" to the wolves and turned women into loving ladybugs, Grace couldn't help but startle whenever she heard it. Ally didn't bat an eye. She was used to it. Aunt and niece talked enough that Ally was used to it.

"Georgia, how are you getting along? Sorry, all. I've been here. I couldn't figure this Zoom thing out, though. Think I've been on mute for about ten minutes. Mom, Raymond and Wes send their love. I was told to tell you their dad's Internet is ... Hang on, I want to get this exactly right ... 'actual crap.' That's what they said. Or else they'd be here." Ally glanced at the other participants. "Peter!! Oh, I wish I could give you a hug. I haven't seen you in forever!"

"I haven't seen *anyone* in forever, it feels like," Peter replied. "Once I get out of quarantine, I'm gonna hold you to that hug, sis. You, too, Georgia."

"What the hell are you quarantining for, anyway Pete?" came Greg's voice. His face filled Grace's computer screen.

Why does he always look so angry? Did we teach him to be that angry?

"Because I was *told* to quarantine, Gregory, that's why."

"Do you always do everything everyone tells you to do?"

"When my life depends on it, I sure as hell do."

"Who says your life depends on it?"

"Let's see," said Peter, and Grace knew her list-maker was preparing the list in his mind. "There's the CDC, the World Health Organization, The State Department ... I could go on."

"Could you really?"

"Boys!" Grace broke in. "It's Christmas. Will you please give it a rest? For me?" She didn't mean to plead, but she sensed she did. Still, if it took pleading to shut them up ...

"He thinks I want to be here, Mom," said Peter in a cross between disbelief and end-of-his-rope frustration.

"I'm not the one who went to Costa Rica!" Greg shot back.

"This was supposed to be a *vacation.* Do you know what those are, Greg? You work all the damn time."

"I work all the damn time to support my family. Life is easier and a hell of a lot more fun when you can do whatever the hell you want. Isn't it, Georgia?"

Grace couldn't believe what she was seeing and hearing. Was Greg really hoping to involve his own daughter in this squabble?

"Greg, I don't want to fight with you. Not on Christm—"

Peter's face hung on the "m" sound. The others waited a long moment before realizing he'd frozen. Ally let slip a tear without, it seemed, knowing it had fallen.

"Oh, Peter," she said.

"Are we supposed to open presents over this Zoom? That could take a year and a half," Greg bemoaned.

"Exaggerate much, Dad?" said Georgia.

"Well, I mean, if we have to wait for Peter's damn third-world Internet, we'll still be here next Christmas!"

Grace thought just then how, if everyone were gathered at the original McCoy home together, enjoying Camp McCoy as they should have been, she'd ask them all, "Who wants pie?" Year after year, that would put an end to any argument. *After all*, Grace mused, smiling inwardly to herself, *be it pumpkin or apple who could argue with pie?*

Peter's face had disappeared after he froze but was back all of a sudden about half a minute later.

"I don't know how long I've got, everybody. The connection is tenuous at best. I just wanted to tell you all I love you." He paused. "Even you, Greg!" Peter smiled. He knew calling his brother out was likely to rile him again, and Grace figured this was her younger son's intent.

"Before you go," Georgia cut in, "I have something to share."

"Oh?" said Grace, intrigued.

Georgia was an artist, but Grace doubted she'd share a picture; she could message over any pictures she painted to anyone in the family and receive an instant reaction. *This must be something else.*

"What have you got, sweet Georgia?" Grace asked.

"It's a poem. I think ... I think it's kinda fitting for today?" she said, a degree of uncertainty filtering through her words.

"Ooh, let's hear it!" said Ally.

"I'm all ears," said Peter.

Greg said nothing.

"Gregory, would you like to hear your daughter's poem?" Grace prompted.

"I would," Greg answered finally, in a tone that belied his true feelings on the subject.

Georgia Grace cleared her throat. "This poem is for my family on Christmas," she read and then looked up at the screen again. "Seeing as we can't actually *open* presents together this year, I thought maybe I could do something different? I ... um ... hope you guys like it."

"Who We'll Be
Who we are this Christmas is not who we will be.
Who we were then is worth remembering.
Who we'll be next season, it's hard for us to know. But
When again we can take the leaps of life,
We'll learn and love and grow."

Georgia looked away and down, shy now. She fiddled with the hem of her Christmas pajama top.

Grace and Ally and Peter all began to clap as one. Yet Grace knew the reaction Georgia was waiting for was her father's.

A reaction that didn't come.

"That's beautiful, Ms. Georgia," said Peter. "I love the way you write."

Her aunt followed with, "Will you send me a voice-message of you reading that poem, sweetie? I want to send it to Raymond and Wes. They'll love it!"

Grace hated how she always had to prod her eldest along, but such was her lot in this later life. "Gregory?"

"What?" Greg said simply.

"Your daughter just recited a poem for all of us."

"I heard it."

"And?"

"And you and Dad taught me that, if I don't have anything nice to say, I shouldn't say anything at all."

"Asshole!" Ally whispered, not quietly enough. She knew the pronouncement would turn her mother's cheeks crimson. Clearly she didn't care.

"Your daughter is talented, Greg," offered Peter. "Why can't you just be supportive?"

"I am supportive," said Greg.

"Could have fooled us," said Ally.

"Am I supposed to tell her everything she does is the next great thing in painting or literature or poetry or slam poetry or pastels or whatever form of art she chooses to dabble in? It feels like it changes every month."

"Dad, what the hell?" Georgia said through a trickle of tears.

"What do you have against your daughter creating, Greg?" Ally challenged.

"Nothing."

"Bull," said Grace and Peter simultaneously. Zoom wasn't sure who to focus on, so it chose neither. The picture remained on Greg.

"Do you guys want to know why I'm not falling all over myself every time Georgia finishes a project or a piece of writing or a diorama of the city?"

Grace nodded. "I think you owe Georgia at least that much, Gregory."

Greg heaved a big sigh. "Fine. I'm afraid, okay? I'm afraid for her."

"What?" said Ally, unsure if she'd heard right.

"Are you ...?" said Grace, still trying to comprehend her son's admission.

"I mean ...?" said Peter, whose Internet was still just on the edge of usable.

"Why would you be afraid for me?" said Georgia, still sniffling. "That's like ... so weird."

Greg stood from his desk chair, left his camera's frame a second. Grace knew he was doing what Greg always did when challenged. Ever since he was little. Before responding to any challenge, Greg would do what his father had advised him to do: "Gather yourself, son. Breathe. Regather. Shake your body out beginning at your arms, moving to your shoulders, and ending at your head. Then, when your initial anger is all chased out, come back and face the world."

"Is it weird that I want the best for you, Georgia?" asked Greg, resuming his seat.

"No, Dad."

"Do you think I work all the time because I love it?"

"Well, we figured you didn't hate it," Peter quipped.

"Thank you for that, Peter," Greg said, with the patented McCoy-family sarcasm. Turning to his daughter's section of the screen (he actually moved to the right in his chair to face her on-screen image more fully), he went on. "Georgia, whether it's fair or not, you need money to live. And while I have no doubt your artistry is real and that you're good, and even if knowing that makes me happy whenever I get to see the newest thing you've produced, and even if I think it's great ... artists and creatives are at the mercy of a fickle world. People may *like* artists, but people *need* doctors, architects, lawyers. They may not like when they have to see a corporate council like me, but they need us. They *pay* us because they need us. If everyone else in your life is gonna tell you your art is great, then I guess I need to be the realist in the group. I don't like doing it, but someone has to."

Georgia stared hard straight into her phone's camera. "You think my stuff is great, Dad?"

Greg was silent for a beat longer than anyone else thought comfortable. Peter thought his brother had frozen. Then Greg said, "Well, not *all* of it. But a lot of it is great, yeah. That poem was pretty good."

"Oh, Dad." Now Georgia was crying again, but these droplets had a different meaning to them. "How come you've never told me what you really thought? How come you never told me any of this?"

Stolid, stoic, starched-collar Greg had to work hard not to get emotional himself. He fought back a lump in his throat. Swallowed hard to get it down. "I wasn't gonna be the one to give you an unrealistic vision of your future, even if you're the best writer at your high school," he said.

"The best ...? Oh ... Well, I just won another award for a short story I wrote about Grandma and Grandpa, and how she and I were with him at the very end."

At this, Grace beamed, Peter gave a pixelated thumbs-up that made it look like he was flipping them all the bird, and Ally said, "Wow! That's so cool! Send it to me, Georgia. I want to read that ... like ... now!"

"What I'm trying to say," Greg continued, "is that I know how good you are. You're my daughter, Georgia Grace. How could you be anything but great?"

Her father was the only person she let use her middle name in normal conversation. Partly because he did so sparingly and partly because it was his mother's name, and she would have felt like an awful person if she'd ever told him he couldn't utter it.

"The thing is," Greg went on, "there're so many Georgia Graces out there. And when you get to college in a few years, you're gonna meet your people ... writers, painters. Hell, you might even get into sculpting. Who's to say? And those people will either encourage you—if they're good people who are kind—and you'll encourage them back. Or they'll try to tear you down, if they're insecure, like your dad," Greg admitted. "I just want you to know that."

"Oh. But, Dad, I ... I also wanna study and work. I just don't know what I want to do yet. Maybe art, maybe languages ... I don't know."

"Oh," Greg parroted. "Well, then that's good, honey."

Georgia sniffled loudly. "Can I come up to your office and give you a hug?"

"My door's always open," Greg replied. "You can come in anytime. Just like you used to when you were little."

Grace wiped her eyes. Ally was doing the same. Peter, in contrast, smiled wide.

"What a cool Christmas," Peter said. "I only wish I was there with all of you."

Georgia climbed off her bed. "Although, if we'd all been together like we usually are this time of year, I never would have written the poem!"

"Silver linings," said Grace. "Now, who wants pie?"

They all laughed.

"We don't have any pies, Mom," said Greg.

"I don't think any of us do," said Ally.

"Of course you do!" Grace replied. "This is still Christmas—a McCoy Christmas. And that means pie." She beamed. "You all get to open your gifts from me now."

"We do?" Georgia said, with, Grace noted, the same excitement she sported every year.

"You do."

Each took their box sent to them by Grace—Peter was surprised his had even arrived at all—a couple of days before. Faces, young and old beamed. Paper flew across screens, discarded and unwanted now that it had done its duty of protecting and decorating gifts, of tempting the future recipients.

First Georgia, then Ally, and then Peter, and lastly Greg—saving the paper dutifully—pulled open their little boxes.

Lids were tugged up and off to reveal the golden temptations within. "Oohs" and "aahs" caressed Grace's ears, and they were in every way as genuine and as real as if the McCoys had all been in the same room together.

God willing, we will all be together next year, thought Grace. But still this was good.

"Oh, Grandma!" Georgia chimed in first.

Seeing her granddaughter's face, Grace knew she'd done good.

"Mom!" Peter exclaimed. "Are you kidding me? How did you get anything through customs?"

"Oh, Mom," Ally said, choking a little sob.

"Nice one, Mom. This is a work of art!" Greg was the first to remove his apple pie ornament from its box and display it for all to see.

Grace chuckled inwardly at her son's choice of words. A *work of art?* Maybe, maybe not. She was not the family artist, after all.

To Georgia, Grace had sent a peach pie ornament. "In honor of ..."

"My name, I know. I love you, Grandma."

Ally grinned wide at the depiction of her favorite pie, pumpkin. With a dollop of whipped cream in its middle.

Peter's ornament was the most abstract. A chicken pot pie hung from its loop.

"Mom, what's this? A chicken pot pie? Why?"

"It's what I'm going to cook for you, my son, when this is all over and you're back home with us."

The McCoys were silent a moment. Outside Grace's window, a light snow fell.

"I don't know who we'll be tomorrow," Georgia said after the pause. "But I know who we are today, and I'm glad for who we are today."

Greg nodded. Ally and Peter did so too with enthusiasm.

"Exactly," Grace said. "Merry *McCoy* Christmas, everyone."

A WINDOW INTO THE FUTURE

The man looks unkempt, his hair going every which way, his beard too long and on the verge of out of control. He wears sweatpants and a ratty old white t-shirt with nothing on it. When he gets home, my book clutched tight in his hand, my signature on its title page, his wife will throw the shirt away without telling him.

Who am I kidding? This guy doesn't have a wife. He probably doesn't even have a home. But he's here, at my signing. A fan. A fan of *mine*. When he gets to the front of the line, I'll be cordial. I know how to do that. I might be quick to dismiss him once he's gotten what he came for. The line is long and this event was only supposed to run for two hours, yet I'll be cordial. The grandmother who raised me would insist upon it.

***

I'm used to being asked for my autograph. And not just by the UPS guy, to sign for the latest among a series of fruitcakes my so-lovable-but-quickly-losing-her-grip-on-reality grandmother's sent me to mark the coming Christmas holiday. Grandma has a plum tree in her yard, so I can bank on at least the plums in those cakes being fresh. The plums are almost worth it. But I end up having to throw out the cakes, anyway, because the jams in the back of her pantry, with which she augments the cakes, are almost surely lethal.

I'll pass, but thanks for the thought, Grandma.

The next time I'm in Seattle, I'll have to check in on her; I'm betting she won't be living on her own much longer. It will be on me to make other arrangements. I'm in L.A. now and will likely need to delay whatever book I'm writing and halt the business of publishing for a time when that inevitability rears. The business of life is, after all, more important.

Beyond signing for parcels containing inedible cakes sent with love, there's also the requisite signing of restaurant receipts, the signing of my ballot every election—to clarify to the powers that be yet again that, no, I have not voted Republican. But I used to give out my autograph so much more, before the pandemic. As part of my day-job. Which I still can't believe *is* my day-job.

As a kid, I remember waiting in long lines when my favorite authors came to town. Visiting our local bookstore. I could hardly believe I'd get to be *in the same room* with them! My heroes! That same fruitcake-sending grandmother—her black hair done up, her makeup on-point—would take me to get their latest book signed, and I'd be one amongst a throng of kids my age clamoring for attention from a man or woman more accustomed to dark rooms and pens, pencils, or time spent on computers than to communicating with readers.

When I became a published author myself, a dream of mine since forever, my grandmother wholeheartedly supported me.

"I bet one of these days, you'll write my favorite book ever, Jack," she once said to me on our way home from a meet-the-author excursion, adding that she didn't know what it would be about because I hadn't written it yet but she was sure I'd do it.

With her support and encouragement, I made book-signings a focal point of my work. Yes, the most important thing for a writer to do *is to* write. You'll get no argument from best-selling author Jack Townsend on this point. The second most important, though: engage with the people who buy your books or ... who knows, next time around, they might not be there to engage with you, and they'll be far less likely to part with their money to see what you have to say. When my first novel came out, and when it hit the way it did—which surprised everyone, most of all me—I told my publisher it would be perfectly fine to book me in every city where they could manage to find a willing bookstore who'd host me. This worked out great for them; at that point, any bookstore owner with a beating heart would have had *the* Jack Townsend in their store to sign books and give talks and just generally be in their presence.

That's what happens when you write a best-seller like *A Window Into The Future.* Gushing over the book invariably turns into gushing over the author.

It's a little hard to get used to, if I'm being honest.

What was even harder to get used to, however, was losing access to these signings and those gushing moments when the pandemic told us all to go home and stay there until we were told to come out of time-out. Even now, if you want to get your book signed by best-selling author Jack Townsend—I promise that is not how I, Jack Townsend the person, think of myself—you need to show your vaccination card at the door to prove you won't infect the unsuspecting and cause death-by-book-signing.

What an odd time in which to live.

If only I'd had a window into the future and bought stock in Zoom, a company that, strangely, has absolutely nothing to do with transportation, and a boatload of stock in … believe it or not… toilet paper? (I'm still questioning that one.)

After all, being a best-selling author doesn't necessarily equate to being the best-known author. Nor am I yet a particularly financially stable author. My bank account is the saddest thing I've ever read. Meaning what goes into my bank doesn't stay there long. Best-selling author Jack Townsend has bills to pay and mouths to feed.

Best-sellerdom these days only equates to being well-known in certain specific circles of a world that devalues literature a little more with each passing day.

***

This store is tiny. A little independent operation done up for Christmas with lights and wreaths and poinsettias tastefully deployed throughout the space. (The café is most of this place, but the bookstore portion is, as my wife would say, "super-cute.") I hope it will still be in operation when I come back through here in a year or so on my next book tour. I don't give them great odds, alas, but passion counts for a lot, and these owners—an elderly couple who each stake out a front shelf with their favorite books, declaring so with fun signage that reads "Bert's Bets" in a flowing red script and, next to it, "Florence's Faves" in orange—they have as good a shot to make it as anyone. From what I can see, Flo is into horror and good ol' Bert is a man after my own heart, prizing the kind of books that promise a good cry. Maybe gender norms would tell you it should be the other way around, but then gender norms are stupid, so I say good for those two. They're happily spending their Saturday at their bookstore. I'm an author Bert recommends. *A Window Into The Future* "made me cry like a baby," says Bert's recommendation. "When I closed it, I was so happy."

"When did you know you could do that, make someone cry?" he'd asked me when I first arrived for the signing. I told him I wasn't sure, but if I figured out the exact moment, I'd be sure to let him know what it was.

I hope when my last page is written that I'm as cool as Flo and Bert—married forty years and living a dream with the person I love.

The store's manager is their son, a bespectacled twenty-something—they must have had kids late—named Brian. It was Brian who arranged this signing, my publisher tells me. "Brian called us and said he *needed* you at his parents' store. That there were bigger stores, more established stores, but if he didn't get you to come and visit, he'd regret it *literally* forever."

So many people, literally, both misuse and overuse the word "literally."

"You see," Brian explained to my publisher, "it's my dad's seventy-fifth birthday soon ... he was a Christmas baby, and he rarely ever got a party like the one I want to throw him because when you're born on December 21, all of the friends who would come to your party are out of town for the holiday ... I can't imagine a better present for him than a book signing with *the* Jack Townsend. I have to make it happen for him."

When my publisher, Will, told me about the call—first in an e-mail, then in a text when I asked for more information—I knew two things: one, Will gets calls like that every day after *Window* came out (he never used to bother me with things like that before because he didn't have to bother me with much of anything before). I also knew that, two, I'd do the date here at Flobert's Books, even though it's in some small town in the Midwest, a town I couldn't name if quizzed. I dare not turn down any chance to sell more books.

I also now know that this state is full of wheat and the traffic's measurably better than back home in L.A. Here, we're able to move, unlike in L.A., where I'd settled when I was sure my life in American letters was dead and I tried to write scripts to support my family. My wife, Claire, is a beautiful brunette, and our kids, Caleb at four and Tess just two (a hard birth, at the beginning of the pandemic's lockdown).

Writing scripts meant I could feed my young family. Any script; it didn't matter what. If they paid, and if I could use that legal tender at any participating McDonald's to get Cal a happy meal and to pay for the formula Tess would need, I'd write the damn thing, no matter how awful the show.

But the sad truth was most of my ideas for scripts would be rejected by the shows' head writers, leaving me working for Lyft to lift my income. Working nightshifts and fitting in writing spec scripts while in the car between rides, which left me shattered and unable to give Claire and the kids the time and attention they needed. Sure, she was understanding. At first. She's always tried, but everyone changes as they get beaten down by life. Just like the characters we put on our pages.

And then *Window*, the novel I'd been writing on the side for years, changed everything. For me, for Claire and the kids, and for Will, the British friend-publisher who'd taken a flyer on a guy who couldn't get a single agent to commit.

"I know how good this book is, Jack," Will had said in our weekly writers' group two years ago. We call that time B.T. or "Before Tess." That Tuesday turned out to be pivotal.

"Any chance you'd let me publish *Window*, Jack?" Will had wondered aloud in the midst of a conversational lull. Everyone else in our enclave knew now was not the time to talk. Negotiations were underway. They waited, silently cheered us on. For a writers' group that had been held at one of four houses each week for five years now, each of us writers (or publishers) at different spots in our respective careers, our first lockdown-meeting on Zoom was looking rather fruitful.

I considered Will's proposal. *Window* had been rejected more than thirty times, basically ignored by anyone who was anyone I'd ever sent it to. And he wanted to publish it? Sure, he'd read it. The whole group had read it, and critiqued it, and they'd been sad with me when nothing came of it. Will was probably just pandemic-drunk, hungry for anything that even resembled literature to nourish his reader's brain. I know I was. If I had to watch one more episode of *Tiger King ...*

"If you want it?" I replied. A question.

"I want it," Will declared.

"Then what the hell? I say let's do it!"

The entire writers' group—all four of us—celebrated that night.

Two years later, here I sit, finally a best-selling author, talking to eager readers at Flobert's Books. When the signing is over, Brian has asked that I stay for cake.

"It's not fruitcake, is it?" I'd said just about twenty minutes ago, when Brian came to tell me the crowd was finally beginning to thin, and that it looked like we'd be able to end the signing on time, while also getting to everyone who wanted a sixty-second chat with best-selling author Jack Townsend.

"No, it's not fruitcake. It's my mother's gingerbread cake. Made right here, in-house."

"Gingerbread cake, huh? Well, okay." I'd smiled, and Brian went to tell his dad the good news. Jack Townsend, best-selling author, was going to eat cake with them. And so was I.

It's so weird that someone I don't know wants to eat cake with me. Sometimes *I* don't want to eat cake with me.

***

Unkempt Rattyshirt is lying in wait.

That's what it looks like, anyway. If he's got a book for me to sign, he's hiding it well, and he isn't eager for our interaction.

That's good. Neither am I. The guy's a little creepy.

Authors need safe words. We'll share them with our hosts, the bookshop owners and store managers. That way, if ever we sense our safety is in jeopardy during a signing, we can alert someone who can help; get the word out without spooking the offending patron.

Leave it to me to forget to share a safe word with Flo, Bert, or Brian today.

This place is so cozy, with its tight quarters, numerous teeming bookshelves containing countless tomes of myriad genres. From mystery to thriller to fantasy to humor to poetry to "Voracious reader Bert's favorite kind of nonfiction: Historical Biographies." The real draw of Floberts, though, and the shop's moneymaker, is its coffee shop (at least twice the size of the bookshop itself). The cakes Flo bakes, says Brian. The gourmet coffee Brian brews, says Bert. The shop is a true all-family concern.

Now it's those same tight quarters decorated for both Christmas and Bert's big day—and my lack of a suitable safe word—that have my heartrate increasing steadily. I'm handing a middle-aged woman back her copy of *A Window Into The Future* and realizing that, after her, there isn't anyone between me and Unkempt Rattyshirt. I look around for either Flo, Bert, or Brian, but I find none of them; they must be in the coffee shop. The plan was for me to finish the signing, send all customers to young Nora at the cash register, and when the last of them had gone, it would be time for cake.

Simple enough, right?

You would think.

"I just loved your book, Mr. Townsend," says the middle-aged woman. She's a curly-haired blonde with her hair swept over one eye. I don't think she can see out of that eye, and my apparent stalker has placed himself in what must be this woman's blind spot. Using her deficit to his advantage.

"Thank you so much," I tell her, trying to play it cool. "But please, Mr. Townsend was my father. Call me Jack."

She smiles. "Thank you, Jack! It was worth waiting in this long line to get to talk to you."

"You flatter me. Have a good night and drive home safe."

"You get home safe, too," the woman counsels. "We gotta get you back to your computer so you can write more books." She pauses. "Oh ... and, Jack ... one last thing? My friend Marci—we're in a book club together—she will absolutely kill me if she finds out I got this close to you and didn't ask … Have you started writing the sequel?"

"I have started," I whisper to her conspiratorially, as though she and I are the only two people alive who are aware. In truth, I whisper this answer to anyone who asks. What I don't tell her is how afraid I am. I'm not just *scared*, either; I'm genuinely terrified. I have written a book in *Window* that hit, a story people wanted. But other than the writing part, I don't know how I did it. I don't know what crazy calculus made my book sell when so many others didn't. And there is absolutely no guarantee I can do it again. What if a one-book wonder is all I am? I guess we'll know in about a year.

"I'm so glad. Another book from Jack Townsend!" With that, the woman is gone, off to get rung up by Nora, and I do my best to shake off the anxiety I've been trying to hide from.

***

After a beat or two in which no one is in front of the table where I'm stationed, Unkempt Rattyshirt at last approaches. Still no book in hand. This guy doesn't care if he *buys* a copy of my best-seller, let alone if I sign it.

My publisher, Will, told me yesterday, "I hate saying this 'cause I don't mean to put any pressure on you or anything, Jack, but there's no way around it. You, my friend, are the author of the moment. What do you think of that, mate?"

Right now, what I think is how that doesn't matter to this guy. I do sense he has an agenda, but I can't begin to guess at what it is. Besides money. He probably thinks I've got money, and a lot of it.

If so, he's wrong, and I hope to disabuse him of this notion.

He steps up to me and just stands there.

Does he think we're having a stare-off? Clearly, I'll need to speak first.

"Would you like me to sign a book for you?" The unspoken question: "Why don't you have a book for me to sign? There's an entire table of them just over there. Brian arranged a big display."

"No," said the man. His voice is gruff, quiet but forceful, almost hoarse.

"Well, if you don't have a book for me to sign, then I'll have to ask you to step aside for any other customers who might want me to—"

"There isn't anyone else," he interrupts. "I waited until there wasn't anyone else."

Indeed, he has. Damn it.

I nod in acknowledgment of this. "How may I help you?" Good. I'm cognizant of striking just the right tone here. If this guy's as off his rocker as I think he is, I have to do everything I can not to provoke him.

"I have a question for you," says the man.

I sit forward, portraying an eagerness I don't feel. Sometimes, posture is everything. My dad once said that body language can make or break a moment. And sometimes while doing this whole thing we call life, you can't help but sense a foreboding. I sense one now, a darkness descending among the place of light that is Flobert's Books.

"Why did you steal my story?"

"I'm sorry?"

"My question could not have been any clearer, Mr. Townsend. But I'll repeat it, in case you didn't hear me the first time."

I get the feeling this guy rehearsed what he had to tell me last night and on his afternoon journey to the bookstore. What he says next is anything but rehearsed, however. It's the real him, and it proves to me he's becoming unhinged.

There's no more dangerous man than an unhinged man behind the barrel of a gun. He points that barrel straight at me.

"Why in the *fuck* did you steal my story and pass it off as your own, Mr. Townsend?"

The gun begins to shake in his hand, and the man glances over at a shelf next to two tables. All brimming full of new, hardcover copies of *A Window Into The Future* by an author about which the New York Times said, "This is a new and welcome voice! Townsend singlehandedly reinvigorates in readers the hope that American fiction is again on the rise!"

***

Plagiarism? He's accusing me of *plagiarism*?

I have done nothing of the kind. I *never* would. Such an accusation cuts at the very marrow of who an author is; the good ones, anyway. Because the good ones are smart, original (even in their retellings of familiar tales), and the good ones listen to their readers and learn what they want while never expressly performing fan-service. I am a little worried about the guy pointing a gun at me right now, though. To say he seems unstable would be charitable. The shaking gun is the obvious sign, of course, but beyond that, the guy keeps shifting from foot to foot, looking around furtively to see if anyone's noticed him yet. Besides me, no one has.

Which may be the only reason he hasn't used that gun on me to this point. Other than he's talking bullshit.

Is it loaded ...? I can't gamble that it's not so I'll have to comply with everything this guy wants, at least until I can summon help.

"What do you want?" I ask. Why put this question off any longer?

"What do you think I want?"

"I don't know. That's why I asked y—"

"I want credit, goddamn it!"

Keep him calm. Let him think he's in control, Jack. That's the only way you'll maintain control of this situation.

"Alright, alright, credit. I understand."

"Do you?"

I don't, but if the crazy, unkempt, ratty-shirted guy with the gun knew that ...

"Sure, I do. What's your name?"

Establish a rapport. Good idea.

"I'm not gonna give you my name, Jack!"

"Why not?"

"Why would I do that?"

The gun is waving around again. Every time it comes back towards me, seated in my chair behind the table, I do my best to lean out of the way of any prospective bullets. But if this guy decides to fire, I really have no defense. I'm a gonner, a sitting duck.

"I give you my name," he says, "and you'll give it to the police. And they'll protect you, Mr. Best-Seller. Don't think I don't know how the world works! I've been living and writing in it just as long as you have!"

Try and connect with this guy on a personal level, Jack. "So you're a writer, too? Just like me!" I say, with fake enthusiasm and an even faker smile.

"Save it, Jack."

"Save what?" My own life? I'm trying.

"That buddy-buddy tone you're using. It's a bigger load of bullshit than that damn book!"

Nora at the register is done with the last of her customers. There's no one else in the store. Everyone else is congregating (and getting a little loud now) in the coffee shop. I need to get Nora's attention any way I can. How has she not looked over here the entire time I've been getting lightly accosted by an armed psycho?

"Don't be trying to escape, either," the man says, sounding out of breath. "You're looking for an escape route!"

"I wasn't."

"I can see it in your eyes, Jack! The way they're darting back and forth! You lie to me again, you'll leave me no choice but to shoot. You got that, buddy?"

"I got it." I lower my eyes to the table. In It, I can see the reflection of the handgun thanks to the table's cleaned-for-a-best-selling-author sheen.

"We need to move," the man decides.

"I'm sorry?"

"We need to get out of here, Jack. That's what we need to do. Yeah. Remove any temptation for you to make a scene. I want you to get up slowly, very slowly, and come around the table to me."

"That's not protocol, sir. If you want a picture with me, we can arrange it. But I make it a point not to touch anyone I don't—"

"I don't give a fuck what you make it a point to do or not to do, Mr. Author. I'm telling you to get your ass up and come around this table to me, Jack. And you better do what I tell you or ..." He looks down at his companion. "Or my friend here will have something to say about it!"

"Alright, alright." I rise and come around to him as requested. He gets behind me and sticks the muzzle of the gun deep into my back.

"Head for the door!" he commands in a whisper. "You got a driver?"

"I do."

"Good."

As we pass by the register, Nora looks up. Is she Flo and Bert's daughter or just a random college kid who loves books?

Weird thoughts occur to you when you realize each thought you entertain might be your last.

The gun has left my spine (I'm grateful for that), and now it only hovers near it. Mr. Unkempt Rattyshirt is distracted, staring at the stacks of my book. They may as well be omnipresent here. He's staring with one part longing, two parts utter contempt.

When the black-haired Nora meets my eyes, I mouth, "Call 911."

Nora stands for a long second, unmoving. Her mouth is an expressionless line. She hasn't finished counting the day's till, and it's likely I've made her lose her place in the count. It couldn't be helped. I'll apologize to her later.

"What's wrong?" she mouths back.

I angle myself so she can better see the man with the gun behind me. She leaves the register and begins a full sprint towards the coffee shop's mirth. She is no doubt about to oust that feeling when she relates the danger best-selling author Jack Townsend currently finds himself in on Flobert's watch.

***

What in the hell is my driver's name? I met him at the airport yesterday, and he told me, but as much as I want to remember it right now, I can't. My mind is crowded with other, more important things.

Like how not to die.

It's a "T" name. I know that much. Tom or Thomas, or Tim or Timothy, or something? Is my driver the kind of guy who would go full name or would he shorten it?

"Sir, I didn't expect to see you so soon!" T-name gets out of the car and is instantly at attention. "Weren't you going to stay for the birthday party?"

"My plans have changed," I say, before my captor has to yell the exact same phrase or, worse, turn the gun on T-name right here.

"I understand," says T-name. "Where, may I ask, are we headed then? Back to your hotel?"

Hell no. The last thing I want is for this psycho to know where I'm staying. Although, I have to consider the possibility that he may have been stalking me for days in anticipation of this very encounter, so he may already know.

"No," I answer. "Can we just drive around for a bit?"

Just as I did for Nora, I angle myself so my driver can clearly see my captor.

Get on your radio and get help, T-name. But first ... get us out of here before we both get blown to bits in the damn parking lot of this charming little bookstore and coffee shop with Christmas lights and so many wreaths hung about its exterior. It won't be charming any more if two people die here today. It'll become the stuff of urban legends, passed by and talked about in hushed voices amongst Halloween trick-or-treaters far into the future.

"I suppose," says my nonplussed driver.

We get in.

My captor isn't nonplussed, but he does have a couple demands of his own.

"So when you get to be a big-shot author, they let you ride around in limos, I see. Well, before we go anywhere, I'll need you to close that divider, Jack. The one between us and the driver. We don't need him eavesdropping on us."

I nod.

"Driver, can you close the divider?"

Without a word, my T-named driver rolls up the divider. Then he sends a text to my phone, which pings when it arrives.

Thompson (Driver): You need anything, Mr. Townsend, just tap on the window and I'll lower her down.

Unkempt Rattyshirt doesn't like where my attention is.

"Hey, best-seller, you should be focused on me, big-shot." The gun is at my temple now. Mr. Unkempt cocks the hammer. "I'm the guy with the gun, don't forget."

"I'm focused," I say, too fast, willing the tremor in my hands to stay out of my voice.

Once he knows he has my attention again, the man seems to relax a bit. He sighs. I read that sigh as his first outward display of satisfaction in my presence.

Then he says, "*A Window Into The Future*. Quite a title, don't you think?"

"I do like it," I say and tell myself not to be cocky. But if he likes it, what's the harm in telling him the truth here?

"Thank you. I came up with it," he says.

No, he didn't.

*　*　*

My publisher, Will, came up with it at the end of one of our marathon Zoom calls. The plot of the book involves a man, Jeff Truman—I'm unapologetic about using what are referred to as self-insert characters in my writing; Jeff is a stand-in for his creator, at a crossroads in his life. Should Jeff stay with the woman he loves, forever wondering and likely never to find out if she loves him in the same unconditional way he loves her but knowing their relationship is marked by its being unremarkable yet safe? Or should Jeff take a chance, break away, and go out on his own? Jeff is afraid of ending up alone if he throws away the safe path he knows how to walk, but he's also afraid of never possessing the gumption to take a chance. The same gumption his pioneer great-grandfather showed when he led a wagon train to Oregon. For Jeff, the story of his family's wagon train was bedtime fare, a tale told by his proud father. As an adult, he revisits that story from time to time, thanks to a scrapbook his mother put together over many years.

Unsure what to do, which path to tread, Jeff chooses neither. He's stuck. It is only when a mysterious stranger shows up at the body shop where Jeff works as a mechanic that Jeff is given any guidance at all. The stranger tells Jeff he isn't a stranger.

"Not in the way you think of strangers, Jeff. You haven't met me yet, that's true. Before this day ..." The stranger squints into the too-hot, too-bright afternoon sun. "Well, before this day, I hadn't met you, either. But now that's all changed. Now you're on a collision course with me. Destined to meet me in your future and my past."

"What?" Jeff doesn't understand. He understands which wrench to use when, which screwdriver is needed for this job or that. But a stranger in his body shop who appears to be talking in riddles ... that he doesn't get.

"It's quite simple, Jeff. I'm here to give you a window into your future, if you have the balls to look through that window. Do what I say and you have *a chance* to live the life you've always dreamed of. Send me away and you'll forever wonder, What if?"

After a fair amount of machinations, not to mention the middle-of-the-book reason why boy can't be with girl right now (that seems to lengthen every "weepy" since a girl from Radcliffe named Jenny told Oliver Barrett III, incorrectly, that "love means never having to say you're sorry"), our man Jeff learns there is a girl for him outside of his comfort zone, and, with the counsel of Future Jeff, our Jeff goes for it with her at just the right time. And life works out right where it should.

On the very last page of the book.

My original title, *A Confused Life*, had confused Will, and everyone else who read the story. They had no idea what to expect from the work and, as such, most of my beta-readers hesitated to open the manuscript. Some who did open it nonetheless could not find their way past chapter one.

"Your story is these two guys, Jeff and Future Jeff. Don't you agree, Jack?" Will had asked me over Zoom. I sat in my rather spartan writers' den—no distractions, Townsend; you're here to write, so write—feeling particularly sorry for myself. A title for this story kept eluding me, despite my months-long continued attempts to wrangle one.

"Yeah. I mean, at its heart, you're right. The story is those two."

"The title seems obvious then," said Will. "It's right there in the story."

With that, the title that had already dawned on Will finally dawned on me. And I call myself an author!

"*A window Into The Future!*" Will and I both shouted in unison. Then we laughed together. Sometimes, as a writer and a publisher in the umpteenth hour of revision and editing, you just can't help it.

The fact that this book for which we'd struggled to find a title (before the perfect title came along and basically fell on us) became an instant best-seller shocked and overwhelmed both author and publisher. But that's what happens when your weepy makes Dena Banks, a famous actress with an even more famous book club, weep into her red wine. Then she tweets and instagrams and does all the social-media things no author should need to know anything about because all they are is distractions. And, over a weekend, your life goes from boring and unremarkable—your desk cluttered with pages no one wants to read—to being asked onto national TV morning shows, for interviews on NPR, and this is your tenth book signing in nine cities in twelve days.

If I told you that best-selling author Jack Townsend were tired, would you believe me? The crazy thing is, it'll be another month or so before I see my first royalty check.

If I'm still around to collect it, that is.

"You came up with that title, huh?" I humor Mr. Unkempt. "*A Window Into The Future?* Then I suppose I should say thanks. Dena Banks told me it was that title that made her pick up the book on her vacation. So ... without you ..."

"Shut up!" His trigger finger looks itchy.

Shut up I do.

He's choked up suddenly and says, "You think I'm crazy, don't you?"

"Crazy? No. Not ... not crazy. Just ... in need of some help."

"I had Jeff's story before you, you know?"

"You did?"

"Yeah. It was all written-out on these index cards my girlfriend bought for me. She always told me my plots were complex and that I'd do well to figure out which scenes I absolutely *needed* in my stories and which I could, as she said, 'confidently cut.'"

This guy has a girlfriend? As of when? My best guess: 1992. In second grade. At recess.

"Well, all I can say is that writing success comes differently for each writer. At different times. In different ways. It's unfair to judge yourself and your writing ability against another author's success. It's most unfair to you. Half of trying is failing. More than half, if you're a hitter in baseball ..."

"Oh, spare me the platitudes, Jack!" Now he's pointing the cocked gun at his own head. "Have you not figured out who I am yet?"

I didn't know I was supposed to be figuring out who he is. "No." I am honest with him.

"I'm disappointed in you, Jack," he says.

The real question is: Who does this guy think he is? Whoever he thinks he is, that's who he wants me to believe he is. Think fast, Jack!

"Are you someone who's come to show me a window into my future?" Maybe he'll appreciate how meta that would be.

If this guy's my future, though, my life's going to turn as bleak as a Dickensian workhouse.

"See, I knew that's what you'd think, Jack, but no, no. You have it wrong. And I'm out of time! I can't wait around for you to figure this out. So here ..." He digs into his pants pocket and fishes out a folded piece of paper, hands it to me. "Read this when I'm gone. It'll all make sense once I'm gone."

"Gone? No, wait. Let me talk to my driver ... Thompson ... up there. We'll figure out a way to get you some hel—"

Before I can finish, Mr. Unkempt fires the gun into his left temple. His head flies back with the blast.

I hammer on the divider between Thompson and me. He lowers it.

"Yes, sir?"

"I need help!"

"With what, sir? Would you like to go back to the bookstore? I've been on the phone with a man named Bert for the last ten minutes. He wants to know if you're alright."

I'm not alright! I just saw a man kill himself in front of me!

I want to say this because it's what I should say. I want to tell Thompson to call 911. But the phrase won't come.

I look to where Mr. Unkempt has been sitting. We shared the black leather bench-seat. I expect to see the husk that once was Mr. Unkempt staring back at me, dead-eyed. I expect to see blood-spatter consistent with the kind that occurs when a distraught man blows his brains out in a limo.

There's none of that. There's no him at all.

I unfolded the piece of paper the man who's no longer here handed me. It reads:

Hello, Jack:

You think you know me, but you don't.

You think you're better than me, but you're not.

I fought the same demons you fought, Jack.

The world believes you won. I'm not sure. I didn't know it was a game. What do you think, Jack?

I'm no window into your future, Jack. There's no such thing. Time travel is a comforting myth. Humans have so little time to spend on this planet. So the idea that we could somehow give ourselves more of what we'll never get more of placates us. It keeps us calm and hopeful.

I'm a window into the truth, Jack. Everyone else—the public, I mean—sees you as the Jack Townsend, discovered and plucked from the slush pile of obscurity by someone so famous you couldn't help but get famous by association. I'm here to show you who you really are, Jack. You see me as unkempt, with a ratty white t-shirt. But think about it, Jack. What do you look like when you're at your computer and you're writing? When you're really in it? Wouldn't you say you look rather unkempt and that you often find yourself wearing ratty white t-shirts with nothing on them? That you look a lot like me?

I am here to remind you how you see yourself, Jack. You're not even sure you belong here, are you? You have a hard time reconciling who you've become with who you really are, don't you? Just some lucky asshole who won a cosmic lottery. And now the memory of me will always be with you, so that you never forget how easily this could all be taken away from you.

Sweet dreams, Jack.

***

When we once again pull into the parking lot of Flobert's Books, Thompson comes around and opens the door for me. I get out and stand on shaky legs.

"Uh, Mr. ... um ... Thompson?"

"Yes, sir?"

"After my signing when I came out and got into the limo ..."

"Yes, sir?"

"Was I alone or was there someone with me?"

Thompson is perplexed. Then he's concerned. "You were alone, sir. I thought maybe you wanted to ride somewhere to get some fresh air."

"I was alone ..."

"Yes, sir. Are you alright, sir? Shall we head back to your hotel?"

"Yes, I think that'd be best."

Just as I'm about to duck back into the back of Thompson's limo, an elderly woman comes jogging out of the store. She's carrying a paper plate and a plastic fork.

"Oh, Mr. Townsend! Is everything alright? Nora told us you seemed a bit out of sorts and that you left in quite a hurry! I'm so glad you came back! I'm Florence! You've met my son, Brian, and my husband, Bert. But I haven't had the pleasure yet, and I wanted to be sure you got a big piece of my world-famous gingerbread cake! It isn't Christmas in our family without my gingerbread cake and a big glass of eggnog to go with it. Here you go! I hope you enjoy this piece of cake as much as Bert enjoyed your beautiful book. Why don't you come inside, and we'll get you some nog, too?"

"I ... um ... cake, right ..." I pause before I manage to add, "I mean, of course, thank you."

Florence turns back toward the shop and I brush my hair back from my forehead. It's getting damp in the light snowfall. I'm beginning to look a tad unkempt, I consider, as I move to follow her in.

THE UNCERTAIN NEW DAY OF HAROLD THE RAINDROP

T he giddy raindrop was excited for his first scheduled trip. At last, he was going to experience the fall for which every young raindrop longed! From the cloud that had been his home forever, the cloud that had nourished and supported him, he'd fall into somewhere he'd never before been.

Would he hit grass or pavement? Soak a smiling face or a woman's beautiful hair of raven?

Our raindrop crawled to the full cloud's edge. He vibrated with nerves. *Maybe I'll hit a nice old lady's hedge?* Then he almost lost his grip on the cloud's fluff—you might think it's made of cotton candy—which would have sent him tumbling too soon, and he said, *I'm not ready to go yet! I haven't yet been assigned a place where I will fall or a falling time.*

His eager pals crowded around him in a line. *It's your turn, Harold!* they said wordlessly, because raindrops can't talk.

Not out loud. They don't have mouths, you see.

Where am I going? he asked with an innocent curiosity the others shared. They, too, wondered where they would go. Whether they'd fall in a steady spring rain or in the winter, windblown.

An old and wise raindrop who'd fallen and evaporated and fallen and evaporated many times over—a veteran of the water cycle—regarded the young raindrop named

Harold and told him, *Don't worry if you feel unprepared, son. At the start, everyone feels unprepared. You'll find your way.*

Change of plans! announced the cloud.

Young raindrops always looked up as they fell, proper and proud, in a spring shower, looking to water a thirsty flower. Colder climates were usually left to the raindrops with experience, but ...

An unexpected wind has blown us off course, said the cloud. *It may not be the strongest wind—certainly it isn't gale-force—but it means you'll be falling somewhere we hadn't expected, Harold.*

Where will I go? said the young raindrop.

The North Pole, said the cloud. *You might even fall as snow.*

***

The cloud drifted right over the spot where he thought Harold the raindrop ought to say his good-byes. Harold wished good luck to all his friends, and he heard the other raindrops' sighs. Harold got to do something fun. When would they? First, before he fell, the other raindrops watched their friend freeze fast, and when he'd fully frozen at last, he let go of the cloud's fluff and tumbled down, down down, not head over heels but head over back.

***

Harold tucked himself up tight. He was now a dendrite. No longer water that would pour in a spring shower; rather—as his cloud had rightly predicted—he was now ice crystals shaped like a six-sided flower.

He heard no sound. No musical fanfare to mark his first fall. No swelling violins.

Nothing but utter silence.

Harold wasn't afraid. In his cloud, he'd hoped and he'd prayed. Now he gave his destination to fate. Until he landed—he'd catapulted from his cloud with great speed but now his descent had slowed to a leisurely rate—until he landed wherever he landed, he'd enjoy the fall, all the while feeling both special and small.

He thought, *I may only be a single flake all alone, but I'll find friends in my new home.*

He'd thought his landing would be momentous. That's what he'd thought when he was a raindrops' apprentice. Instead, he landed on ground soft as a quilt. Little did he know what next would be built.

But first, tired from his travel, Harold slept. The fresh white quilt made certain in good company he kept.

***

When he woke, he found his environment changed. The quilt was gone. Or, more accurately, it had been rearranged. All around him, a group of children who ranged in height from two feet seven to three feet nine, green hats affixed on their red heads, danced around his former bed.

"Wake up, Mr. Snowman," they called.

Harold realized he was standing and that he towered over them, standing at least five feet tall.

But how? I was just one snowflake in search of friends. Look where I am now!

All of a sudden, Harold felt a drop of water in his mouth. *I hope this isn't a trend. I'm a five-foot-tall snowman in an elfin huddle, but if I should melt, all I'll be is a giant puddle.*

"C ... can y-you hear me?" Harold spoke haltingly to the four elf-children who looked at him lovingly.

"I told you he could talk!" said one of the little people with glee.

"How did you know?" said another.

"This place is magic. Or so says my mother. She says it only takes one magical snowflake to make a snowman with whom you can play! What should we do with him today?"

"Have you ever seen a snowman quite like him?"

"I had a snowman once. I named him Jim."

"Sure, but have you ever seen a snowman who could talk?"

"No. For that matter, I've never, ever seen a snowman who could walk! Catch him!"

***

Harold was confused. He was new to it all. The walking, the talking, the being five feet tall. He sensed he was made of exquisite stuff. A group of friendly flakes, who'd banded together and oblivion they magically rebuffed.

"Ho-ho-ho!" said a jolly fellow about eight feet tall. "Who do we have here?"

"I'm ... Harold," he said, but the name felt wrong. That much to the snowman was clear. "I apologize," he went on. "Harold is my name ... when it rains."

"Did my friends build you?" the big man guessed.

"I don't know who your friends are, but I'd have to say yes."

Just then, the little elves caught up to their snowman.

"Santa! We're sorry. He ran away from us before we could give him a name!"

"Ho-ho-ho! They're my next generation of elves," the man named Santa explained. "Many of their parents are elves employed in my workshop, fashioning dolls and soldiers and shelves! If you can talk, that means you, my good sir, are quite rare! Somewhere inside you is a magical snowflake who fell through the air."

"In that case," said Harold, "Harold's not who I want to be. Even if that may be my name legally (although, raindrops have a tough time opening the mail and signing for packages.) If it's all the same to you, could you call me Frosty?"

"Whatever you'd like," Santa agreed. Then he added, "Say, we're just about to make a delivery trip, Frosty. How would you like a ride in my sleigh? Not only will we have fun, but it might keep you from melting away! It gets pretty cold up in the clouds!"

"I get to go back up to the clouds for a visit with my friends? This is the joyfulest news you could convey! And when we are done, our trip all squared away, I'll stand on this big quilt and enjoy my snowman days."

Santa smiled and said, "Then Frosty you'll be, the friend and magical snowman for me, with a song in your name we'll sing merrily."

BONUS STORY
WHAT ETERNITY TAUGHT EVE

The Afterlife is bureaucratic as all hell.

And, while we're at it—not that it's important for this story or anything, but I feel you should know—there *is* no devil. No counterpoint to God bound by and determined on evil. Humans do plenty of evil all by themselves. They don't need help.

If anyone would know this for a fact, it would be me. Hi, I'm Terrence McDonald, curator in the Afterlife's Hall Of Records.

Ugh. I hate that beginning. I sound like an ambulance-chasing lawyer with a plastered-on smile shilling himself on a cheap-ass late-night commercial. And if you disagree with me on that, if you instead think this beginning should be given the benefit of the doubt, you're wrong.

Did I mention that writing stories is hard and the author can often be his or her own worst critic? Yep, that's definitely a thing. And it's definitely a thing *for me*.

Back to my whole ambulance-chaser point. There aren't any ambulances in the Afterlife. (What can I say? God hates sirens.) There're far fewer lawyers in this place than you might think, too, although they all try to litigate their way in. Can't really blame them. It's what they know.

Most in the Afterlife have a job. It's not a requirement and there's no *time* up here exactly, so it's not like you need to put in an eight-hour day or the standard forty-hour workweek to see a paycheck in a fortnight. But eternity is *eternity*, so most people want to have something to do with themselves, just so they don't go nuts.

I've had my job a while now. (Forgive the vagueness of that statement. It is both unintentional and can't be helped up here, since time is a human construct and, for the most part, we don't use it.) As the curator in The Hall Of Records, the largest library ever conceived—and too big to be measured against any other library, biblioteca, bibliiotech, etc.—my job consists of knowing exactly what a soul might need to read, research, or learn about when they come into this Hall. Most times, it has to do with the life they've just concluded living and I can find what needs to be found without too much effort.

But there was that one time ... the time I met Eve.

Honestly, it's the only blemish on the reputation of this Hall since God created all things. I'm still a little perturbed it occurred on my watch. It all started innocently enough with a beautiful blonde making her way through the library doors.

***

For some, there is a certain inarguable artifice to the act of writing. Mainly those who see themselves as belonging to Big-L Literature. Sometimes in life, I'd sense this artifice while reading a book. Most often a classic, but it sneaked into some modern books, too. I would always recoil from this artifice. It made my skin prickle in a not-so-good way. Though he was not a writer per se, my father, Carl McDonald, worked as a professor of American literature, and he prized Big-L Literature; authors who'd use big words to demonstrate their ever-expanding vocabularies; authors who believed themselves above the fray to which most *writers* were, and still are, subjected.

My father and I have always differed in this respect. Where he honored Big-L Literature, supposed sophistication, and the joyless but craft-laden ability to layer words on words on words without ever really saying anything, I was, and still am, awed instead by the act of telling a story. For it is stories—and not large, impenetrable tomes—that can ultimately change lives. Whenever I set out to tell a story, on some level I'm setting out to change lives—or, more accurately here in the Afterlife, souls—as well. How successful I am at this, I suppose, depends on each individual reader who encounters my work.

I hope I can tell you a good story here, dear reader, and that—if I do—you might return to it again and again.

***

She came into the Hall eager. Not surprising. Everyone's eager when they first arrive back Home. That's because any earthly sicknesses or disabilities—whether acquired at birth, shortly after, or along life's long and bumpy road—have been removed upon physical death. Bodies are lighter, as they are comprised in the Afterlife only of the soul and the person's former essence. Minds sharpen. And folks are more than willing to learn.

They all have one question, of course.

What did it all mean?

"Excuse me, sir," the newcomers will often say to me. "I don't mean to bother you." They *all* think they're bothering me, and they're all apologetic.

"You're not bothering me," I'll assure them. "This is my job. Do you have a question?"

"Yes," they'll say.

"Fire away."

"It's a big question," they'll warn, thinking themselves the first to ever come up with it.

"I've heard them all." This is true. I have.

They'll pause then, almost certainly, working up their courage. Then they'll ask it. "What did it all mean?"

At this, I'll ask for their name and their earthly birthdate. They'll give both to me without hesitation because their curiosity overwhelms their sense of privacy; the fact is that—other than working in what looks like an official capacity—I'm a stranger to them.

That's when I'll excuse myself and retreat into a private room within The Hall Of Records that only my predecessors and I will ever see. (I think my wife was in there once, but it's not technically allowed, so you didn't hear that.) In this room, everything that made up a person's life has been stored, cataloged, preserved. Look up a name, discover a life. Simple as that.

Once I've found a person's life in amongst the innumerable lives that have been lived on Earth, I'll return to them and ask if there's anything in particular at which they want to take a look. An incident. A memory. An occasion. Anything that might help them make sense and meaning out of what they've lived.

Most people are a tad timid at first, unsure just how much they have the ability to review. Once they realize the whole of their life is at their fingertips ... that's when it gets fun. It is a joy to watch a soul as they relive their formative incidents—to watch understanding and clarity wash over their whole self.

If I'm being honest, it's the part of my job I most love.

As you've probably guessed by now, though, the blonde girl was different.

What was different? you might be tempted to ask.

Before you do, I'll tell you this: my answer is simple and yet—to me, anyway—deeply frightening.

What was different? *Everything*. Well, everything except …

She approached my desk, not unlike her new-arrival peers. Eager. Eager to learn. Unlike them, though, she wore confusion like an ill-fitting black cloak she wanted to remove but could not, lacking the agency to do so.

She was eager, I realized, to be unburdened of something unseen.

"May I help you?" I started the conversation, as she seemed in search of words that would not come, and we were instant kin.

She took a long moment before answering. Then, in a small, wispy voice, she said, "I hope so. Where am I?"

"This is The Hall Of Records, ma'am."

"The Hall Of … uh …" She was distracted; I was sure she hadn't understood. She began turning this way and that, glancing about, trying to find familiarity in surroundings bringing her nothing but unease.

This didn't happen. People were *glad* to be here. People were *glad* to see me, even if they didn't know who I was. And they never knew who I was, unless I explained it, and I only explained it if they insisted. Maybe one in every five hundred would insist like that. But once I explained the whole thing, even the most cantankerous sorts smoothed out and were fine.

"So you're saying I'm dead, then?" the cantankerous would say.

"You are, yes," I'd confirm.

"Huh."

I've never quite figured out what this little grunt-shrug meant, but it meant *something*. Maybe it indicated that the cantankerous thought there'd be more to the Afterlife? I'm really not sure.

Then, invariably, the new arrival, cantankerous or not, would say, "I'm here for a reason, aren't I?"

"You are."

"What's that?"

"Well, you're a brand new arrival. That means you've died in the last week or so in Earth-time. We don't have time up here. It's a human construct. Have you met with your panel yet?"

"No. Was I supposed to?" Now the new arrival will look concerned.

"Some souls come here first, if they've got a particularly tough loose end to their life they need to tie up or come to terms with. They come here if they need my help getting the knot to that loose end tied up just right, let's say."

That explained why the blonde woman came into The Hall Of Records. Why she approached my desk. Why she did what nearly everyone before her in a similar situation has done. Why she was eager.

What it didn't explain is how her eagerness was different from any I'd seen. Still there with her uncertainty. Reserved, tentative. Or how come this same woman could not remember who she was.

"Who am I?" she asked. Not a query—among the myriad queries—I'd been trained to expect. In fact, this was a question I'd never once heard in my post as head curator at the Afterlife's Hall Of Records.

I tried not to look shocked. Tried ... and failed.

***

Identity is the most basic of concepts. From the day we're born into the human condition, we begin growing into our identity. We're given a name, a date of birth. Maybe a family. Maybe not. Sometimes, we need to find the family to which we're meant to belong. Regardless, we come into the world inherently proficient at certain skills, naturally lacking in others, and needing to be taught how the world works.

This was, and is, true of souls new to Earth. It was, and is also, true of the other realms God created, too. One of the ways my newest world worked was this: even those who passed away with their memories shrouded in Alzheimer's or amnesia retained every one of the memories they'd supposedly lost to time or age or sickness when they returned Home to the Afterlife to stay.

"You look pale," she said.

"I ... I ... what?"

"You look pale. Are you gonna faint?"

"No, ma'am. That is, I mean ... there's no fainting in the Afterlife," I told her, not so confidently.

"I'm sorry ... there's no fainting ... where?"

"You're in the Afterlife, ma'am."

"I'm dead."

That is what being in the Afterlife is meant to imply, yes, I think. That's a bit too snarky to say to a new arrival, so I think better of the declaration. But I'm too late to pull it back into my head. She's already—

"How could I hear that? You didn't say a word just then—your mouth didn't move. But I heard ..."

"You heard what I was thinking."

"Yes."

"It's telepathy, ma'am. We often use it here in the Afterlife." A pause. "Sorry. I can imagine this is all a bit of a shock. It certainly was to me when my passing came."

She steps back from the desk. "I ... I need to sit down."

"Of course." With a quick flick of my wrist, I put a chair directly behind her. She all but fell back into it. "There you go, ma'am."

With that, I came out from behind my desk to join this lost soul at the table closest to her newly relocated chair. I moved another chair—this one manually, no wrist-action involved—over to the table for myself.

"Can you give me your name, ma'am? If you can give me your name, I can—"

"I can't remember my name."

"You can't ..." I couldn't help fidgeting in my seat. *This has never happened before. Not ever.* "Okay," I said, attempting to regain my composure. "We don't need your name. We can use your birthdate. Can you remember that, ma'am?"

"I can't remember *anything!*"

"Nothing?" I said, panic beginning to rise within me, too. But I couldn't show it; I had to remain professional.

"I'm sorry," the woman said, her head in her hands as she began to cry.

"It's okay," I said. Is it, though? I might need to bring The Boss in on this one. We're very near an Afterlife emergency here.

***

The Boss and I spoke regularly as my job demanded it. Usually through telepathy, which was easier for us both, requiring less energy than physical communication. God didn't mind, never has, though he'd prefer spoken language as He thinks it's clearer. But I've done the job enough that I no longer find myself something near starstruck when in His presence. But I'd never called on Him for a situation like this. (I don't think my predecessors in this job did, either.) I'd never told him he *needed* to come to The Hall Of Records to assist with what we call a "transition" from life to Afterlife.

When I did, He obliged, arriving instantaneously. I thanked him profusely.

Still, whenever I mention "the incident in the Hall with Eve," He'll only ever say, sometimes vocally, sometimes through thought: "I did what needed to be done, Terrence. That's all. And what needed to be done was ... an investigation, let's call it."

***

Eve wasn't her given name. Instead, it was the name *we*—The Boss and I—gave her, and to which she agreed, as a placeholder. Until we could discover the real one. And, yes, the Eve reference was intentional, a nod to The Bible. (Which isn't my Bible in the same way it might be yours, or your parents'; I never was super religious, and that's okay, God Himself has told me.)

The Boss introduced himself to Eve. "It is wonderful to see you again, Eve. I'm God."

They shook hands. He was in the guise of a hotel bellman. I asked Him why, whether there was any significance to it.

"Not really," he answered. "Since we don't know who Eve is—or who she was, I should say—I couldn't appear here as someone significant from her own life. A bellman seemed both formal and non-specific. If you think about it, no bellman ever really *knows* who you are; yet, it's their job to be cordial to everyone. I suppose I could have also chosen a restaurant waiter, but a bellman will do."

This type of declaration epitomized The Boss I knew. He tried with all His might to be exacting. And yet, He would make mistakes of tense. He'd begin a phrase with, *Eve is*, only to remind himself that, as far as Earth was concerned, whoever Eve *was*, she wasn't that person anymore, her former self now a mere shell, a carapace.

It was both refreshing and off-putting to be reminded of God's imperfection.

"Isn't there some record of my passing somewhere up here?" Eve put in. "There has to be, right? I mean, okay, I don't know my name, and I don't have any memories of life, but my passing had to be *expected*, right? I mean, You knew I was going to pass." She turned in her seat toward The Boss. "You knew I was coming Home, even if I might be the first human in history to have forgotten herself in the Afterlife. Right?"

God sat back in His seat at the table, impressed. "Whoever you are, Eve ... whoever you *were*, that is, there's no doubting you must have been quite intelligent. That was a cogent argument."

"Thank you." Eve smiled weakly.

"I'm just sorry it's wrong."

"Wrong? Why is it wrong?" Eve challenged.

Only now did I see that God brought with Him a briefcase. (Did He bring it with Him, or did it only just appear, out of thin, you-don't-need-to-breathe-it-to-stay-alive-up-here air?) Out of it, He took a single sheet of paper and laid it on the table.

"Read this."

Both Eve and I leaned forward to do so. I couldn't decipher what I was supposed to from the paper, though; its print was so fine as to strain my now-perfect Afterlife eyes.

"What does it say?" I asked. "I can't read it."

"Neither can I," Eve seconded.

Oh, good. It's not just me, I thought.

"It says that, on the previous Earth-day, a total of 212,000 humans came Home to stay."

"That means they died, right?"

"That's right, they died. And every single one of them was welcomed back Home by a loved one."

"Every single one?" said Eve, in an almost-whisper.

"That's right."

"But I wasn't. Why wasn't anyone waiting to welcome me Home?"

With a sinking feeling in my now-too-full-though-never-expanding stomach, I answered Eve's question. "No one was waiting to welcome you Home because whoever you are, Eve, you ... weren't supposed to come Home yet."

"I knew there was a reason we made you the head curator of this place," The Boss said. A compliment perfectly delivered as it came across in the way that

133

allowed my soul to accept it most readily: veiled in sarcasm.

After a pause, I ventured, "I don't know that the three of us are going to be able to solve this mystery." Working alongside an imperfect Boss, an imperfect God, was one of the things I'd learned about him. He wasn't much for puzzles—they frustrated him. As they frustrated me. The Boss was all for philosophical conundrums, and He could explain them when one-on-one with a soul. But Eve's case seemed weightier. I feared if we didn't bring another mind into our think-tank, all thinking might stall. The Boss did not contradict this thought.

"You have an idea of someone we could bring in to help?" This was a question, not a statement. Not uncommon for The Boss. He didn't mind asking questions. And besides creating the world, at which he can only be described as *expert*, he was—and remains—adept at delegating.

"As a matter of fact, I do," I said.

***

Patricia was my spirit guide. Which is to say: when I lived on Earth, this black-haired beauty served as my conscience.

"How does one get to be a spirit guide?" I asked her not long after I returned Home to stay and took up my post as curator of The Hall Of Records.

"It takes much dedication and a dedicated soul. Being a spirit guide—working as a conscience—is pretty much a thankless job."

"How so?" I'd asked, the two of us seated at my desk in this very library.

"We make suggestions. That's really all we can do, since The Boss decided free will should determine who does what when on Earth and that any judgment for those actions comes later, once a life is lived. As all we can do is make suggestions ... it follows that those suggestions will often be ignored."

"And they are?" I asked. "Ignored, I mean?"

"Oh, more often than not, yes."

Patricia paused. As she did, I sipped from a can of Coke. The sweet potion glided down my Afterlife gullet. (The best thing about the Afterlife: folks can eat or drink anything they want and never once worry about gaining any weight, always remaining at what was long ago on Earth determined to be their ideal weight. My doctors had told me to stop drinking Cokes when I was somewhere in my forties. And I had, always the dutiful patient. Besides, if I'd tried to sneak one, my wife, Mattie, would have had my head. But now that I'd returned Home, as it were— now that I was well and truly dead—no physician's advice was going to keep me from this blissful sugar-water. My former favorite soft drink. I may have singlehandedly kept the local Coke plant in operation as a teenager.)

***

Patricia arrived at The Hall Of Records, said a cheerful yet serious hello to The Boss, and met Eve.

She reminded me of the conversation we'd had an eternity ago. I hadn't exactly forgotten it, but so much had happened in my job. Moreover, one of the joys of Afterlife living is how you can forget things that don't matter in a given moment—how the only thing that matters is what's happening right now—so I'd shuffled this conversation to the very back of my mind, as part of an uncluttering. A practice not uncommon for me.

"Do you remember how that conversation ended, Terrence?" Patricia asked me.

"Um ... well, no, not exactly," I admitted.

"That's ironic, since it's probably the reason you called for me to consult on this case."

"Do tell," I said.

"Yes, I'd like to hear this, too," said The Boss.

"Okay, I will," Patricia agreed. "Since everyone up here knows a spirit guide's suggestions will be so readily ignored, The Boss gave us another job to do when we're not quietly advising within the minds of humans."

"What's that?" Eve asked.

"Spirit guides are incredible researchers. If there's a mystery that needs solving up here, all you need to do is get one of us on the case. Eve, I'm confident I'll know who you are in no time."

No matter how long it took to determine Eve's identity, since there's no time up here, what Patricia said was true. (A little Afterlife humor for you.)

***

I used to laugh at my dad, Dr. Carl McDonald, PhD, when he'd sit for hours in a library researching something. Did he think this was an efficient way to learn about a topic, crawling through hour after hour of microfiche? The Afterlife, like life before it, is ironic. Now I was seated next to Patricia, Eve, and The Boss Himself, searching the seemingly endless records in this expansive-doesn't-touch-its-scope library.

"What are we looking for, Boss? If Eve wasn't among the souls returning Home, what could her reason for being here possibly be?"

God was perplexed, too. He rubbed his bellman's temples to try and stave off an onrushing headache. I wonder if God only gets headaches when he's in a human guise.

"We're looking at the visitors list," He said.

"The visitors list? What's that?" Eve questioned.

An appropriate question for her to ask, I thought. I know what the visitors list is, but that's because it's part of my job. Terrence McDonald *better* know what the Afterlife's visitors list is! Eve, meanwhile, wouldn't. And shouldn't, as it's part of the Afterlife's bureaucracy: humans are not expected to concern themselves with our particular brand of sticky red-tape, considering how much they're bound to have to cut through every day they spend down on Earth.

"Every Earth-night," The Boss explained to Eve, "approximately one thousand humans visit us up here in the Afterlife. As Earth is always spinning, the sun is always shining somewhere on Earth, and it is also dark somewhere on Earth at all times.

"So, if you figure that a thousand visitors appear up here each night—their business here ranging from simple chats with a deceased loved one all the way up to preparing them for a soon-impending death, and everything in between—it means that, at any given untimed moment up here, there are approximately five hundred visiting souls joining us in the Afterlife."

"Do you think I'm a visitor?"

Now Patricia took the reins of the conversation. "It's a theory," she said.

"But if we don't know my name, how can we possibly expect to find me among a thousand visitors?"

"The advantage of the visitors list," Patricia answered, "is that it has pictures to help those of us in the Afterlife recognize each and every visitor. It also lists the reason for each visit and the duration of that visit. The visits themselves take place at night so they can be explained away as dreams when the visitor awakens back on Earth."

As the four of us spoke, we stared closely at a screen not unlike those used to display microfiche many decades ago on Earth, except that this microfiche was Heaven's own technology (there is even an audio version, but Patricia, like me, could be described as old-school). Patricia was constantly rotating the archive, in a slow, measured motion, as though she'd been trained for the work. Which she had. Now we knew of what we were in search: if Eve was on the visitors list, somewhere among all these pictures and life-statistics—which looked not unlike the meat of obituaries—we would find Eve's smiling face, accompanied by her actual name.

Eve looked disgusted as a thought came over her. I could actually see when it dawned. "If there are pictures to help identify each and every visitor, why not each and every returning soul, too?"

This was a question for The Boss. He fielded it gamely. "What can I say other than the Afterlife I created is bureaucratic to a fault?"

"Not good enough!" Eve shot back.

"Actually it is," I said, reaching up and placing my hand on Eve's shoulder, the same way my own mother used to when she was attempting to calm me.

"What do you mean?" Eve turned her moistening eyes on me. They were blue, and unlike the hard-as-flint orbs The Boss saw, these were soft and pleading.

"Departures and returns—births and deaths—are closely tracked up here. With two-hundred thousand people returning to the Afterlife each Earth-day, and twice that number departing for life down on Earth, we *must* have a much better handle on who's coming and going.

"Everyone arriving Home will be met by loved ones, as we told you. Everyone departing for Earth—their former loved ones will see them off."

"Which means," God said, "there's no need for us to include pictures of those arriving in or departing from the Afterlife. Much easier to produce a thousand pictures a day as opposed to six hundred times that number."

***

It might have been minutes. More likely, it was hours. Since we don't keep time up here, it's impossible to know. But, at some point, Patricia cried out. A sharp intake of breath. A tiny but unmistakable scream.

"I think I've got something!"

"What is it?"

I wasn't surprised that Eve was the first among us to speak upon this declaration. She was, after all, the person our little research project concerned the most.

"That's your picture, isn't it, Eve?" Patricia paused our search on a photograph—or the Afterlife's facsimile of a photographic image—of a woman who did resemble Eve. If you looked past the bags under her eyes. The hair, apparently unwashed and certainly out of place; she hadn't seen a shower in days. The expression she wore was as far from a smile as an expression can wander. Haggard, tired, spent, frowning.

The perfect time to snap a photo, I thought sardonically. "If that's you ... I don't mean to be rude," I hedged, "but you don't look good."

"Sometimes, seeing a picture like this one will bring back memories for some souls," Patricia said.

"Does that picture jog your memory at all, Eve?" The Boss asked.

Eve sat silent and gazing in at the woman she was, or the woman she'd clearly been once. As we continued to stare at it, any residual doubt left us all. This *was* Eve in the picture.

"I'm sorry, I-I still can't remember a thing!" Eve buried her face in my chest, and I hugged her to me.

It wasn't usual for me to take such a personal interest in the souls who came through The Hall Of Records. As a rule, my job comes with a level of distance to it. Once a soul has a brief interaction or two with me, they're on their way, and if I see them again I might not even know it, since I work with so many and since the entire populace of the Afterlife has probably been in my presence over the course of my work. But no soul had ever been so lost when they requested my help as Eve was.

"No need to apologize," Patricia assured her. "All of these visitor photos come with their own set of identifying information. It looks like ... yes, see there." Patricia pointed again.

Pointed at a mystery solved. An investigation completed.

According to the photograph's stats, directly underneath it—which reminded me of the back of a baseball card—the woman The Boss and I named Eve as a placeholder was actually:

Name: June Carol Travis, née Crawford.

Age: 28 yrs.

Marital Status: Seven years married to her husband, Paul David Travis, a major in the U.S. army.

Reason for visit: Mrs. Travis is visiting as part of a "dream" in which she will meet her son, Joshua Nicholas Travis.

Suddenly, a pained look ruled Eve's—June's—face. "No, that can't be right!" she shrieked.

Neither Patricia nor I—heck, not even The Boss—understood what had June up in arms.

"We solved the mystery, Mrs. Travis," Patricia said.

When June rose and threw her chair aside, retreating to a far corner of the Hall, Patricia swiveled around in her own chair, got up, and followed. As did The Boss and I, though we stayed a fair distance away, though just close enough to still hear what was being said between the two women.

Once a writer, always a writer, I thought. And a good writer knows how to eavesdrop. I smiled to myself at this. Terrence McDonald, curator at The Hall Of Records and master eavesdropper.

"I-I can't be here to see Joshua!" June cried.

"Why not?" Patricia asked, her tone kind, not dissimilar from that which she used with me when I first met her, a six-year-old kid trying to keep his parents from getting a divorce. I met her in a dream of my own.

A dream that wasn't exactly a dream.

"If I were here to see Joshua, that would mean ..." We all watched as the realization broke her. "That would mean ..." She fell to her knees. "Oh, God, that would mean he's dead!"

This was not something she'd just learned. Rather, it was the last fact still to be shielded by the memory loss that had beset June when she first arrived in the Hall. According to June Carol Crawford's vital stats, which all four of us read, her son, Josh, had lived only ten days. His heart too large, his little body kept functioning with the aid of machines and tubes running through it.

The loss was fresh. The little boy had only returned Home a week ago. After his death, June had been rightly inconsolable. Had used a number of sleeping pills to combat her newest companion—insomnia.

"If only I could get to sleep ... I-I wouldn't have to think about how I'd lost my boy. How he'd died as I held his little hand."

Now that The Boss knew who June Carol Crawford was, he stepped forward. In the guise of her father.

"Junie, he's not dead, you know?"

"He's not?"

The Boss shook Frank Crawford's head. "No one *ever* dies. They just come Home, that's all."

"Well, I won't let you have him; it's as simple as that!"

"Is it?"

"You're the one who gave my Joshie his bad heart. You owe me time with him!"

"I gave you time with him," said The Boss in her father's most soothing voice.

"Ten days with tubes running in and out of his poor little body is hardly a life!"

"Would you rather he hadn't existed at all?"

"No! Of course not! But I never wanted him to be in pain the way he was."

"No parent—if they're good at it and compassionate and they truly love their children unconditionally—no parent ever wants their child to experience pain. But they're going to, Junie. Whether they live ten days or eighty years, pain is assured."

A bout of silence settled over our group. My former spirit guide broke it.

"How much time have we got?" Patricia asked suddenly of no one in particular.

June turned an accusatory look on The Boss. "I thought you said there was no time."

"Not up here there isn't," He replied. "But you're sleeping down on Earth, Mrs. Travis, scheduled to wake in an hour and a half. Now that we know you're here to see your Josh, we need to make it happen ... and quickly."

***

It was decided—amongst the four of us—that I would escort June to meet her little boy.

"You've been with her since she arrived," Patricia reasoned. "It should be you who introduces her to her son."

The Boss concurred wordlessly. I blushed with honor.

"Does it matter where the meeting takes place?" I asked.

"I don't see why it would," said The Boss. "Pick somewhere you like."

***

That's how June Carol Crawford and I ended up in what I've called Pondering Park since I was on my own Afterlife visit at six years old. The park is vast greenery, its impeccable grasses varied and growing unhindered by any blights or pesticides that might spell doom down on Earth. The two of us sat at my favorite Pondering Park bench.

June turned to look at me. "Thank you for all your help." Tears tickled the edges of her eyes but would not fall. Yet.

"Of course, ma'am. If I'd realized we were on a timetable ... That happens so rarely up here ... Plus at first I thought you were a new arrival, not a visitor, in which case time would not have been a factor. I'm sorry."

"You have nothing to apologize for, Mr. McDonald."

"Terrence. Please call me Terrence."

Just then, she brightened. Leaped to her feet. "Terrence, someone's coming! Is that ...? Is that my Josh?"

Across the varied uber-green grasses of Pondering Park strode a blond-haired, blue-eyed boy of about ten. He wore a suit he clearly found uncomfortable, and he kept tugging at it; maybe it was itchy, but he wore it, anyway. This was a special occasion.

"But ... how is he so old?" June asked. "He's a beautiful boy, don't get me wrong. But why is he—"

"Returning souls can choose to experience the Afterlife at any age. Your Josh must like the feel of being around ten years old."

This I knew June would remember as long as she lived. And, on the boy's tenth birthday many years hence, there would be an extra-special celebration in the Travis household: a *party* as opposed to the usual somber remembrance. And two cakes.

When he got to within arm's length of June, he stopped. Along with the suit, I noticed, he wore the kind of pants and dress shoes no little boy of ten would ever wear of his own accord.

"Josh," I said, shaking the little boy's hand, "my name is Mr. McDonald, and right here is your mom. She's been waiting a long time to see you again."

Josh quickly broke our handshake and went for a hug from June. From his mom. Whom he'd never called Mom. She took him into her arms readily. He fit there like the missing puzzle piece that made her a whole person again.

"I've missed you, Joshie," she said. "My little angel."

"I've missed you, too, Mom," he replied, his words half-buried in the black blouse she wore. Black was the color of grief, of grieving, and she'd never stopped.

"You have to live your life, you know," Josh said to her when the two were finally apart.

"I do," she told him.

"I'm okay. And I'll be okay whether you're happy or sad, Mom. So you might as well be happy."

"Was there anything I could have done?"

"Done?"

"To save your life? To keep you down on Earth with us. It's not just me that misses you, you know? You're our whole family's angel."

"And that's what I'm supposed to be. That's *why* I was supposed to be."

"What do you do up here, Joshie? When we're down there just trying to find our way through the days, what are you doing up here?"

"Lots of things," he said and seated himself on the bench.

"Name one," June challenged. "Tell me one thing you do up here. Can you do that for me?"

"Sure, Mom. Well, I'm getting my sister ready to go down to Earth and join you."

"Your ... *sister*?"

He nodded. "Her name's Emily. You can't meet her yet, but you'll see her in about eight months."

June looked down at her belly. Not yet swollen. "Eight months ..." she said, almost to herself.

I felt a little guilty eavesdropping now, but every story needs a proper ending. My father, the professor of American literature, would agree with me on this point.

"Will I ever see you again, Joshie?"

"Of course you will, Mom. You'll see me when you come Home, but that's not for a while. And, just so you know, whenever you or Daddy talk to me, I hear you. I know sometimes you wonder if you're talking to thin air, talking to nothing. You're not. When you talk to me, I'm with you, Mom, and I'll always be. I'm your angel, right?" He grinned up at his mother. "If there's one thing we angels learn up here, it's that an angel's work is never done."

June's face reddened. "It's not ... *enough*," she said.

I thought about breaking in, giving a more detailed explanation of the way things worked up here. If anyone could give a detailed explanation, it was me. But I sensed this was young Josh's ground to trod. No one else's.

"It has to be enough, Mom," he said.

"Why?"

"Because it's what you get. It's what we got. It's *all* we got."

"Well, what if I don't like it? What if I'm grateful for what we got but it still makes me mad to know we could have had so much more?"

Josh took a long pause before saying, "That's okay, Mom. It's okay to be mad because it's a human emotion. Be mad. Be angry. Feel everything. That will help you mourn me, but it will also ready you for the new soul you'll be meeting soon."

Now I broke in. "I'm afraid our time is coming to an end, Mrs. Travis."

Both she and Josh instantly knew what this meant

June looked up at me sadly. "But ..."

I nodded a little. "I know."

They hugged once more, the little boy who was not dead, just Home, and the grieving mother who'd been instructed to choose *living* over grieving.

I think they might have said goodbye to one another, but if they did, I didn't hear it. Then, before they could separate again, June Carol Crawford disappeared off my favorite Pondering Park bench, coming out of a dream-state and awakening into a new Earth-day.

Find out how Terrence wound up working for Heaven
in the award-winning *What Death Taught Terrence*.

To find out more about the novel, head to the "Also Available"
section at the end of this book.

THANKS
FOR READING

Thank you for procuring and reading this book. We hope you enjoyed it.

Remember *Fifty Shades of Grey*? 'Twas good ol' word of mouth that spread the word for that. It's *you*, the *readers*, that are the lifeblood of publishing. Honest reviews encourage readers to check out and buy books! Sales enable writers to write the stories you read ... Simple!

So, if you did enjoy the story, please consider letting others know, won't you? A brief review—even just a line or two—& rating on your bookseller site and/or on Goodreads can mean so much to authors and independent publishers. Scan the QR codes to go directly to Goodreads and Amazon.

Thank you *so much*!

Scan here to go to **Goodreads**

Scan here to go to **Amazon**

AUTHOR BIO

Derek McFadden is an author, a poet, a podcast presenter, a radio enthusiast, an unapologetic fan of the Seattle Mariners, and a former March of Dimes ambassador.

He lives with a mild version of cerebral palsy, and his eyes aren't great at being eyes.

Derek's acclaimed novel *What Death Taught Terrence* was a **Next Generation Indie Book Award Finalist 2021** and the **Best Adult Fiction Winner** at **The Wishing Shelf Awards 2021**. The audiobook version, read by the acclaimed BJ Harrison, was a **Best Adult Audio Book Finalist** at **The Wishing Shelf Awards 2021**.

Derek's second novel, *The Santa Claus Agreement* was published in 2022, finally lifting the lid on exactly how Santa Claus works. A **Wishing Shelf Awards** "listed title," it debuted to rave reviews ... just not enough of them. We blame Santa and his conspiracy of silence.

ALSO AVAILABLE

What Death Taught Terrence

Rated **4.5** stars (from 54 ratings) on Goodreads
Rated **4.5** stars (from 53 ratings) on Amazon

The TV is on, and I'm on the couch, leaning as far back as I can. My heavy, indecisive brown eyes—their lenses blurred ever since my tumultuous, too-soon entrance into the world—flutter between open and shut. I am half-watching, half-listening to a football game on a Sunday afternoon. Was that the doorbell?

"Who is it?" I call out, expecting to hear my daughter, Megan's, voice. These days, she is the one person who visits me. The only person who knows I'm making my home in this little oasis fashioned from wood felled by my own hand.

"Terry, it's Mom. I'm here to help you move."

My mom? That's not possible. She's ...

Wait. To help me move? Oh, God.

I rise from the couch and glance back at my lifeless body.

Life is a journey. So is the Afterlife.

At the end of his life, Terrence McDonald must discover its meaning, or he'll be banned from the Afterlife forever, and his soul will cease to exist. Join Terrence—and those who love him—on a poignant and unforgettable journey through a life at once wonderful and harrowing. Learn what Terrence learns. See what Terrence sees. By this provocative story's end, readers may even learn a thing or two about themselves.

Winner, The Wishing Shelf Awards, 2021
- Best Adult Fiction

Finalist, The Wishing Shelf Awards, 2021
- Best Adult Audio Book

Finalist, Indie Next Generation Book Awards, 2021

"The question is not What Death Taught Terrence, but what Terrence, the engaging protagonist of this story about the Afterlife, taught me... McFadden shows how learning to look beyond outward appearances not only enriches our understanding of others but also deepens self-knowledge... McFadden presents the reader with an extraordinary gift: insights into empathy, a most rare commodity today."

Amazon Review

Find at all good booksellers in
hardcover, paperback, e-book, and **audio**

Turn the page for a QR code direct to Amazon:

Praise for Derek McFadden's award-winning
What Death Taught Terrence

"What Death Taught Terrence offers a powerful, painful, and poignant look at the life of a man rarely encountered in fiction. Derek McFadden's writes with an insight few can match."
– T.F. ALLEN, author of *The Night Janitor* and *The Keeper*

"A good story allows the reader to experience life as another person, and McFadden made me do so on a deeply personal level. If you like the works of Mitch Albom, I think you'll find What Death Taught Terrence a worthy addition to your library and the reading of it a life-affirming journey."
– BRADLEY HARPER, Edgar Awards finalist and author of *A Knife In The Fog* and *Queen's Gambit*

"In what Death Taught Terrence, Derek McFadden builds a world that satisfies both our desire for imagination and our need for personal introspection. I found this (story) immediately immersive, and it stuck with me long after I finished. McFadden is doing something rare in today's fiction—exploring the limits of what we will believe to form a better understanding of who we are."
– ALEX DOLAN, author of *The Euthanist* and *The Empress of Tempera*

More Christmas fun in...
the *Tinsel & Twists* series

A heartwarming series filled with enchanting stories that capture the spirit of the holiday season. Each tale explores characters' unique experiences of Christmastime. Cozy winter landscapes, twinkling lights, and the scent of cookies baking... Kindness, forgiveness, and the importance of family... Hope and destiny. Each tale reminds us of how "the true meaning of Christmas" connects to us in the modern world.

Strap in for a grand adventure together with Santa's reindeer, enjoy some poignant and uplifting ghostly guidance, and delight in moments of reflection beside a crackling fire.

The *Tinsel & Twists* series will warm your heart and help you snuggle into the holiday season.

Turn the page to find out about the books in the series...

Derek McFadden

Derek McFadden's

The Santa Claus Agreement
A Holiday Fable of Magic, Whimsy, and Heart

Rated **4.5** stars on Goodreads

Rated **4.5** stars on Amazon

A holiday fable chock full of magic, whimsy, and heart, The Santa Claus Agreement *chronicles the adventures of a boy destined for a magical experience… if, all grown up, he can keep his end of the bargain.*

"A holiday story about the search for love and acceptance. Love must begin within, but no one is better equipped to show you how than McFadden's Santa. As a writer and working Santa myself, I can vouch that this story will warm your heart like hot cocoa and chocolate chip cookies beside the fire."

– Bradley Harper, author of *A Knife in the Fog*

Scan the QR code to read a sample or get a copy of the book:

Prefer the audio version?

Find it on Amazon or scan the QR code above.

– narrated by multi-award-winning narrator BJ Harrison –

in **hardcover** and **paperback**, on **audio** and **Kindle**
and *FREE* on **Kindle Unlimited**
(check availability)

https://books2read.com/SantaClausAgreement

And more Christmas fun in...

the *Tinsel & Twists* series:

Will Knight's

The Bear's Last Word (on the matter)

The Christmas presents are gone! The reindeer are missing!
And only one team can save Christmas...

Starring
James J. Jones as "James" and the bear as "Bear"
special guest star Santa Claus as "Santa."

This year there's got to be Christmas!
"We gotta save it for the kids."

Wait... didn't that already happen *years ago*?

Honestly, it's hard to tell when you're old and your adventures are all behind you. Retired from adventuring and now living in a care home, the old bear has this one last Christmas with his best friend, James.

But James has a surprise for his childhood friend and sidekick. It's time their story was told, their old Christmas adventure revealed: What Did Happen THAT Christmas? Journalist Jess Walter has been tasked with the scoop... if there's enough breath still in the old bear.

A poignant "Peter Pan meets Benjamin Button" holiday adventure, Will Knight's *The Bear's Last Word (on the matter)* delivers fun and pathos in spades and tugs at the heartstrings in this final pull of the Christmas cracker for one man's special childhood friend.

Find The Bear's Last Word (on the matter) at Amazon
in **paperback** and on **Kindle** and *FREE* on **Kindle Unlimited**

Scan the QR code to read a sample or get a copy

"A rather different book! Yes, it's fun, whimsical, charming, funny. Yes, it's got flying reindeer, a grumpy dragon (okay, a little unusual for a Xmas story), and mischievous gnomes squaring off with Santa's elves. Yes, there are adventures within adventures, including a balloon trip to Greenland, but this book is as much for the grownups as it is for the kids. It's not just that Mom and Dad are likely to laugh at many of the jokes, it's also that this Xmas tale deals rather poignantly with the mortal affliction of aging as well as with impending loss. I enjoyed it all the way through and was pleasantly surprised when the author threw a final curveball, at which I swung—and missed... A great choice.

Amazon review

All profits from *The Bear's Last Word (on the matter)* are going to **St Barnabas House** hospice (UK).

The Bear's Last Word (on the matter) is also included in the anthology *The Bells of Christmas II*

Turn the pages to find out more...

And even more Christmas fun in...

Lilla Glass's

The Sugar Plum Redux

The Nutcracker *meets* Buffy *meets* Die Hard*... with a dash of Christmas rom-com mixed in!*

Lilla Glass re-gifts the magical seasonal fae The Sugar Plum Fairy. She's all dressed up with some place to go in this deliciously dark comical reinterpretation of *The Nutcracker.*

The Sugar Plum Fairy has a nighttime job helping children get through their nightmares. She slays their demons with her sharply spun popsicle axe and brash attitude. It's all so easy for her until one nightmare proves more than she can handle. She needs help... from *anyone* except her ex-boyfriend! When he takes no for an answer, they set off to help one child take on the Rat King & his cohorts. But a deeper nightmare lies beneath this for one man and his ghosts...

Layered and inventive, *The Sugar Plum Redux* is full of fun and wit and heart for the holiday season.

Find it on **Kindle** and *FREE* on **Kindle Unlimited**
at Amazon

Grab a smaple or copy using this QR code:

This story is featured in the Christmas/Holiday anthology
The Bells of Christmas II
in aid of
St. Jude Children's Research Hospital.

Turn the page to find out more...

The Bells of Christmas II

**Eight Stories
of
Christmas Hope**

– includes –

Derek McFadden's *The Last Christmas Gift*

Will Knight's *The Bear's Last Word (on the matter)*

Lila Glass's *The Sugar Plum Redux*

And **3** entries by Edgar Awards finalist and Silver Falchion winner **Bradley Harper**

Features an all-star cast, including:

The Bells, Santa Claus, Mrs. Claus, the Ghost of Pops, Young Maria, Old Bear, and even Sugar Plum (yes, the fae). Guest starring the Soul of Tintoretto.

"A wonderful collection of eight Christmas stories in one book. They are feel good stories that warm the heart... It reminds you that the human spirit is very kind even during these turbulent times."

"Roll up, roll up, folks! Hear ye, read ye these eight—yes *eight*—stupendous stories we have for you upon this year's yuletide. Come one, come all for tidings of Christmas hope! Savor these dainty dramas and delight in delicious darkness fantastical, with all sure to enchant readers aplenty this holiday season!

"Come, good gentlefolk, as we alight gently on December 24th, the last sleep before Christmas! In Bradley Harper's *The Bells of Christmas* the midnight carols have echoed off into the night as Julius slumbers beneath his bleak blanket, nestled in the bowels of the homeless shelter. A visitor will arrive to make his Christmas wish come true in a most unexpected way.

"Beware, have a care! For Derek McFadden is back among the ghosts in *The Last Christmas Gift*, in which Travis is on the edge of despair while on a most unexpected boat ride. Look yonder, good gentlefolk, for *there*, just boarding... surely not Pops, his beloved grandfather departed these twenty years hence...?

"Now, light ye all *A Winter Candle* as we partake of Bradley Harper's telling of Ben, newly retired from the military. What is an old soldier to do when he feels his family is lost to him? Why, folks, become a Santa Claus, of course! But who is it that detects the faintest flicker of hope in his heart? I tell you, someone up North is watching...

"But lo! Not all these gifts within are fiction. Oh, no, good folks! For within, there sit true-life encounters too. Hear Bradley Harper recount fact stranger than fiction! Hear ye what he's learned in *What Santa Has Taught Me*, an essay of experiences as a real-life Santa Claus.

"Good people, come close... let me whisper this to ye... 'Who among us didn't love Christmases when we were all but wee wildlings?' Ah, then relive the magic of your childhood in Maria O'Rourke's *Calling Us Home* as she lovingly recalls the magic of Irish Christmases of yore, where enchantment and excitement were magic unto themselves!

"Will Knight's *The Bear's Last Word (on the matter)* fairly hales at the heartstrings in this final pull of Christmas crackers for one lad's special childhood friend at the "Bears Cares Home." With one last Christmas together, are their adventures truly concluded?

"And now, I ask you all, fair folk: *dare* you encounter the bitter-sweetness of *The Sugar Plum Redux*? Lilla Glass gifts us a fantastical fae, a tenebrous telling of *The Nutcracker* from a very different point of view.

"Ah, but all good things... Yet still one last journey, fair folk, where we must ask ourselves if Gus is not the hero in his own story, then who can it be? Andy, the 'real' and righteous writer? Or perhaps Daphne, the nonconformist neighbor? Before we reach journey's end, Erol Engin will show us how even the most selfish and insecure can provide a Christmas miracle in *A Tintoretto of the Soul*.

"Bless you, one and all, for your forbearance! Click ye a *buy now* button at those most wonderful of shops Amazon, and may your generous soul bequeath donations desired by that most worthy and hearty of hospitals, St Jude! For, above all, 'tis surely the season for children. For who among us deserves magic more than they?"

Award-winning authors Bradley Harper, Derek McFadden, and Erol Engin lead this seasonal collection of magical storytelling!

100% of profits from sales going to
St. Jude Children's Research Hospital

This veritable Holiday treat, *The Bells of Christmas II*, is available for your delectation at:

Amazon

in **hardcover, paperback**, on **Kindle**

and *FREE* on **Kindle Unlimited**

Scan the QR code to read a sample or get a copy of the book

The *Bells of Christmas II* is a beautiful selection of short Christmas stories with all profits going to charity. Each story in this book I found to be great in their own way and as I sat considering how I would review this book I wrote down the 8 short stories and marking down how I scored each one, only to find that I scored each of them 5 stars.

– Feed My Reads (review on Amazon)

"For, above all... 'tis surely the season for children. For who among us deserves magic more than they?"
– Darles Chickens

13 by 11
An Anthology

13 short stories by **11** award-winning and up-and-coming authors

- features Derek McFadden's *What Eternity Taught Eve* -

"An eclectic, genre-busting gathering that will appeal to a wide audience."

– D. Donovan, senior reviewer *Midwest Book Review*

Our human need for connection to others...
in life, in death, in school, in families, in space, in cyberspace.
Even in France.

In part ONE, Vincent Czyz and Derek McFadden ask us to consider the ties that bind and define us in our earthly existence, with tragic, yet hopeful, tales of loss and love.

In part TWO, we visit characters at different stages of life: childhood, early adulthood, and parenthood. Jeffrey Kahrs's charming vignette journeys back to a childhood incident and its effects—both immediate and lasting—on family dynamics, while Caroline Scott introduces us to two teens embarking on adulthood while coping with the pressure of their pasts. Erol Engin warns us how the first child—and Steve Jobs' iPad—can change a marriage, leading to competition and vicarious coping, shall we say.

Be careful what you wish for in part THREE, where enticing temptation meets delicious pleasure, but at what cost? Your life? Your soul? Bradley Harper's dark, tantalizing poems wrap around Lilla Glass's unfurling tale of hunter and prey ... and hunter, before Harper spins a whodunit, with a dash of whimsy and perhaps time travel, if the detective's client is to be believed.

Part FOUR takes us to other spaces. Harriet James shows us the futility of resisting the spark of attraction in a charged love-across-the-divides spec-fiction story. Carla Rehse whisks us off to outer space, where we find two partners, divided in a way we could never imagine, fleeing from a Church determined to part them. Will Knight's dialogue-driven diary tale looks for smiles as it touches on hope vs. reality, even as we wonder what the space of that reality is.

The anthology concludes in part FIVE by considering loss. Bradley Harper's short passage here is a true story, looking at loss of life, while Greg Gerke brings the collection to a close on a pensive note as he describes a gradual loss of self, finding that travel does not necessarily enrich the soul.

13 by 11 is a delightful, engaging mix of award-winning and up-and-coming authors. Together they blend literary, historical, speculative, mystery, and romantic fiction with a dash of light sci-fi thrown in ... but all centering on our human connection to others—in life, in death, in school, in families, in space, in cyberspace. Even in France.

Find *13 by 11* at Amazon

in **paperback**, on **Kindle**,

and *FREE* on **Kindle Unlimited**

"*13 by 11* excels in strong images and depictions that provide much food for thought."

– D. Donovan, senior reviewer *Midwest Book Review*

Scan the QR code to read a sample or get a copy

Derek McFadden

Cover design

Papillon du Père Publishing

www.papillon-du-pere.com

@PapillonPere

Copyediting

Jay Allchin
@ The Editing-Store.com

www.editing-store.com